Wearing only a towel and a killing glare...

The man loomed in the doorway, dripping water. His eyes scanned her briefly, flaring with an interest that struck a responding chord in Liz.

Liz clutched the basket handle tightly, and after her initial quick perusal, managed not to let her eyes drop below chin level. She was here to see Goldie, not ogle this sexy monolith. "Is Goldie here?" she asked politely.

"No-o-o," he drawled, "and neither are the three bears."

Before Liz realized his intention, the door closed soundly in her face. Stunned, she banged on it again. It swung wide.

"Listen, lady, I've got better things to do than have milk and cookies with the neighborhood welcoming committee." He gave her another brief once-over. "On the other hand, if you're the plumber, I think you forgot your tools."

Annie Sims began writing fiction in high school. When interested classmates started demanding daily updates on her stories, she realized she'd found her calling!

She and her husband, Frank, and their two sons now make their home in Oregon, where Annie quickly founded a local Romance Writers of America chapter—Heart of Oregon—and continues to edit the monthly newsletter.

A mother's work is never done.
From that place beyond,
her energy, excitement and
encouragement continue to prevail.
This is for you, Mom. I miss you.

THE
SUGAR CUP

Annie Sims

W🌐RLDWIDE.

TORONTO • NEW YORK • LONDON
AMSTERDAM • PARIS • SYDNEY • HAMBURG
STOCKHOLM • ATHENS • TOKYO • MILAN
MADRID • WARSAW • BUDAPEST • AUCKLAND

Special thanks and acknowledgment to
Ann Simas

RECYCLED PAPER · RECYCLED PAPER

ISBN 0-373-83275-3

THE SUGAR CUP

One

Liz felt a little like Red Riding Hood on the way to Grandma's house. She wore no red cape, and the house she was visiting was Goldie's, not Grandma's, but she did have the requisite basketful of goodies: freshly baked chocolate-chip cookies, a one-ounce bottle of a sinfully sinful French *parfum,* a delicate Italian gold chain and locket, and the latest love story by Goldie's favorite author.

Liz knocked on Goldie's door. A moment later, a movement to the side caught her attention, and she turned to find an enormous golden retriever sprawled on the porch beneath the swing. "Where'd you come from, fella?" Liz asked. She walked over to the dog and knelt to pet him.

The big animal raised his head, enjoying the attention. Liz stood, looking down at him. He stared back with intelligent brown eyes, cocking his head one way, then the other. His eyebrows seemed to arch eloquently, while his tail beat a steady thump, thump, thump against the porch.

Liz shook her head, her expression wry. "I go away for three months and she gets a dog. I should've known she'd pick a golden retriever. That's what she's always wanted." The dog yawned hugely and lowered his big head against his paws.

Liz went back to the door and knocked again. After several more tries, she frowned and put her ear to the wood. Finally she heard a muffled voice. It sounded disgruntled and very masculine. Liz relaxed, a smile on her lips. *Goldie, you sly old girl,* she thought. *Got a fella on the side, huh?*

Liz's smile broadened to a full grin that was wiped right off her face when the door flew open with more force than Goldie was capable of. Liz clutched the basket handle tightly and after her initial shocked perusal, managed not to let her eyes drop below the chin of the man looming in the doorway clad in nothing more than a towel and a killing glare.

His eyes scanned her briefly, flaring with an interest that struck a brief responding chord in Liz. "You're a little old to be selling Girl Scout cookies," he said.

Liz bristled, the absurdity of the situation momentarily lost on her. Thirty was *not* old. She opened her mouth to retort and promptly closed it again. She was here to see Goldie, not spar with this sexy monolith. Her eyes remained studiously glued to his blue ones. "Is Goldie here?" she asked politely.

"No-o-o," he drawled, "and neither are the three bears."

Before Liz realized his intention, the door closed soundly in her face. Stunned, she released a pent-up breath and rocked back on her heels. Without reconsidering, she banged on the door again. It swung wide.

"Listen, lady, if you're here on a social call, you can forget it. I've got better things to do than have milk and cookies with the neighborhood welcoming committee." He gave her the once-over again. "On the other hand, if you're the plumber, I think you forgot your tools."

Liz's temper, usually slow to burn, experienced spontaneous combustion. "I am neither the welcoming committee nor the plumber," she sputtered, as nose to nose with him as a ten-inch difference in height allowed. "I'm here to see Goldie, and if you don't tell her I'm here right now, I'm going to...to..."

"To what?" he asked, in a menacingly soft tone.

"Give you a good swift kick in the shin," she finished with a bravado she wasn't feeling.

His eyes held a glitter of amusement. "Honey, if Goldie was here I'd get her for you, but she isn't." He flicked at a drop of water running down his nose. "And right now, I need a plumber to get me some hot water, not a goofy broad who can't find the right address."

His words and patronizing tone unraveled her. "Honey," she mimicked between clenched teeth, "if you slam the damned door in my face again, the next person you open it to will be a cop."

"Fine," he agreed.

This time when the door slammed, the very walls seemed to rattle on the foundation.

Liz couldn't believe he had done it again. She raised a white-knuckled fist to the door. A thunderous growl preceded its opening.

"Lady, you're really starting to tick me off."

"You're not exactly thrilling me, either!" Liz almost shouted. "Where's Goldie?"

"Who the hell is Goldie?"

"My friend. She lives here." Liz took a fortifying breath, and with it came renewed anger. "You're the rudest person I've ever met."

"Look, lady," he said, running a hand through hair dripping pearls of water down his chest, "*I* live here. Alone. No Goldie. No anyone. Okay? And I can be as rude as I damned well please in my own home."

Liz felt like the main character in Stephen King's worst nightmare. "*Goldie* lives here," she insisted, fighting a surge of unease that seemed bent on turning into downright panic. "Goldie Fabrizio. We've been having coffee and cookies together in this house every Tuesday for years. She *has* to be here."

A subtle change came over the dark-haired giant. His eyes narrowed, but beneath the dark fringe of long curly lashes, he was looking her over again. For some reason she couldn't fathom he seemed to be examining her, not because he was interested in her, but rather, because of something she'd said.

"What's your name?"

Liz wasn't giving out any information without first getting some about him. "What's yours?"

"Jace McGuinn." He crossed his arms over his wide bare chest, apparently not bothered at all by the fact that he was standing there in nothing but a towel. "And you are?"

Suspicious of his sudden concession to polite formality, she gave him what he wanted. "Liz McAyeal." And because she had learned to do so at an early age, she put out her hand.

He accepted it in his own firm grip, but his expression gave nothing away. "Kindred spirits."

"Only if you're Irish," she retorted. His hand was large and had the feel of hard work.

He shrugged. "Too bad. The Scots and the Irish never did get along."

"That's because the Scots are too pigheaded for their own good," she said before she could stop herself.

He gave a chuckle, but Liz was aware it didn't quite reach those blue blue eyes of his. She stared into their depths, mesmerized. She felt as if she'd known him, through his eyes, forever. With a great effort, she managed to tear her gaze away. Awkwardly she cast about for a new focal point, which was difficult, since his well-built frame filled the doorway.

"I guess maybe you'd better come in before the neighbors get an eyeful." He checked the tuck on his towel. "I'll go get dressed."

All the stories Liz had read or heard about perverts and sex maniacs surged through her brain. He didn't look dangerous, but he *was* big. The blue terry-cloth towel draped around his lean hips matched his eyes, but left virtually nothing to the imagination.

Her gaze locked with his. Positive he could read her thoughts, Liz called herself all kinds of a fool. She'd never let a man's looks get to her before. She was more into brains.

"I promise I'm not holding your friend captive in the basement," he taunted. His eyes swept from her hair, which was pulled into a saucy brown ponytail at the back of her head, down across her form-fitting T-shirt and long bare legs, to the pink-tipped toes peeking out beyond the leather straps of her sandals.

Gooseflesh had risen on her arms, and invisible fingers danced down her spine in a purely sexual response. "This house doesn't have a basement."

He flashed her a devilish grin that raised her body temperature and temper simultaneously. Liz didn't trust Jace McGuinn. Not for one minute. He was living in Goldie's house and Goldie was nowhere in sight.

That, and a mocking smile as good as any dare, propelled her across the threshold. He'd tell her where Goldie was or he'd be eating that towel, instead of wearing it.

"Coffee's on," he said, gesturing toward the kitchen as he climbed the stairs. "If that damned plumber shows up, let him in, will you?"

Everywhere she looked, things were different. Gone were Goldie's delicate bric-a-brac and formal cherry-wood furniture. Gilt-framed pictures had been replaced with impressive Gorman prints. The pleasing geometric designs of Indian-patterned rugs made a bold statement on white wood floors that had once been scattered with Aubusson carpets. All the draperies had disappeared, and in their place were miniblinds that let in almost more sunshine than Liz could handle at the moment.

Goldie's two-story Cape Cod home had always been charming, but the metamorphosis from Goldie Fabrizio's style to Jace McGuinn's was more than astounding. It was frightening. Liz fought back the fear threatening to choke the rational side of her, which demanded she wait for explanations.

She came to an abrupt halt in the kitchen archway, where she encountered a cook's paradise. A dozen copper pots hung from a ceiling rack, and several appliances took up counter space that had been pristine for as long as Liz could remember.

If not for the floor plan, she never would have believed this was the same place Goldie had occupied just months ago. There was a warmth about the house Goldie had never quite achieved.

Liz resented it. And she was afraid.

What could Jace McGuinn possibly say that would explain his living in Goldie's house?

Liz decided she must have entered the Twilight Zone. After returning from a three-month sabbatical in Europe, with Goldie expecting her for cookies on this bright summer Tuesday morning, what other explanation could there be? she wondered, fighting the insistent notes of the haunting musical theme as they chased each other around the back of her mind.

She placed her basket on the pedestal dining table. The aroma of freshly ground beans permeated the air. Well, Jace McGuinn had invited her in for coffee, and coffee she would have.

Liz boldly poured herself a cup, but in his absence, she and her bravado crumpled into the nearest chair. *Oh, Goldie, where are you?* she agonized. *People don't just vanish without a word. Especially not you.*

Liz put down her cup. Her head fell forward into her hands and she let herself remember.

Goldie Fabrizio, born Esther Howe more than three-quarters of a century ago, had been affectionately dubbed Goldie by her gangster lover-turned-spouse. Giovanni Fabrizio had loved Goldie's golden locks as much as he had loved Goldie. She had borne him three children in rapid succession before he mysteriously disappeared one Saturday afternoon on his way to confession.

It was anything but okay. Besides, the way he said "lady" made it sound like a four-letter word. "I get the distinct impression you don't like Goldie, yet you claim you don't know her."

His lips tightened, but Liz noticed a slight flush creep up his face. "I may have heard a few rumblings about her."

So he *did* know something. "From your leasing agent?" Liz challenged.

He shrugged, maintaining his stance.

Liz swallowed hard and blinked against the tears scalding her eyes. "Maybe you'd better talk to him again."

With a full measure of dignity, she picked up her basket—and the cookies—and walked out of Jace McGuinn's kitchen, his house and, hopefully, his life.

She felt his blue-eyed gaze burning into her back as she made her way across the wide expanse of grass-covered yard to her own home.

Two

Liz flung her basket inside the front door and took off to pound the neighborhood pavement.

After an hour of door-knocking, one thing was painfully clear. Goldie Fabrizio had lived in the same house, on the same street, for nearly two decades, and not one of her neighbors knew more than her name.

Sticky with her own sweat, Liz plopped down on the bricked steps leading to her front door and cried. She couldn't remember ever experiencing such a feeling of sadness. How could anyone live seventy-six years, almost twenty of them in the same place, and be nothing more than "that woman who lives in the cute little Cape Cod"?

Wallowing in her distress, Liz did not hear the mail carrier approach.

"'Afternoon, Liz. Almost tripped over you." He chuckled, then noticed her tears.

Liz swiped at her eyes. "Hi, Eddie."

Eddie peered out from under the brim of a cap that had been walking the route as long as he had. "You hurt, Liz?"

"No." She choked back a sob. "Oh, Eddie, can you help me? Goldie's disappeared and no one knows where she's gone. And there's some guy living in her house who says he's never heard of her."

Eddie slapped her mail against the palm of his hand. He looked up the street, then down, and finally over his shoulder before turning back to Liz. His voice dropped. "You didn't hear this from me, Liz, but a few weeks after you flew over to Europe, I all of a sudden got a forward on Goldie's mail to a post-office box belonging to some guy named Joseph Fabrizio." Eddie squinted up at the sky. "Now I figure that isn't your most common name, so it's probably a relation, right?"

At Liz's continued look of distress, Eddie snapped his fingers. "Say, I've got it. She used to get a lot of mail from this law firm. Maybe they can help."

She watched as Eddie withdrew a pen and scribbled quickly across a piece of her occupant-addressed mail.

"Don't like it much that Goldie just up and disappeared, Liz. Heck, when your folks went and got themselves killed in that airplane, at least I read it in the paper." Eddie pulled off his cap and scratched his balding head. "I been plenty worried. Called my daughter, who nurses at the hospital. Even been watching the obituaries."

Liz's insides clenched with dread. Eddie had just put into words a possibility she hadn't wanted to think about, let alone admit. Goldie *couldn't* be dead.

Ed shrugged philosophically. "Got to be practical, Liz. Expect the worst, then if the news is good, you get a pleasant surprise, instead of one that's not."

Depression and fear ate at her gut with equal fervor. "Thanks for this name," she told him, pushing herself to her feet. "I'll let you know as soon as I hear anything."

Liz cut across the grass to Jace McGuinn's, even though she'd adamantly sworn to herself she never wanted to see him again.

He opened the door on her third knock. "Damn, I thought you were the plumber," he muttered, but didn't invite her in.

She resolved not to be intimidated as he towered over her in the doorway, his arm stretched above his head, palm flat against the jam. His muscular denim-clad legs were spread apart in a pose that could have sold millions of blue jeans.

"Have you managed to find out anything about Goldie?" Liz asked.

"I don't remember saying I planned to."

"I just thought you might have called your leasing agent or something. I haven't been able to learn anything." She silently cursed the catch in her voice.

His features softened. "Go home, Lizzie," he said. "I'll tell you something when I can."

That was an odd turn of phrase. Liz opened her mouth to question it, then promptly decided not to. Jace McGuinn had made a concession when she least expected it. She wasn't about to risk annoying him.

She pasted on a smile and said thanks, wondering what she had to thank him for as she headed home to change clothes.

The law offices of Osborne Osborne Osborne and Griffith were beautifully decorated, if a little ostentatious.

Chester B. Griffith, the receptionist told her, was the attorney she wanted to see. Chester. He sounded solid, trustworthy.

A tall lean man, his silver hair perfectly groomed and his pin-striped suit perfectly tailored, greeted her. "A pleasure to finally meet you, Liz," he said, taking her hand in his. "I've been trying to reach you on and off for several days—with no success, obviously. Come in and sit down."

Liz had dealt with an attorney only one other time in her life, and that was regarding her parents' estate. She wasn't sure what to expect. "Thank you, Mr. Griffith," she said as he led her to a butter-soft, cocoa-colored sofa and sat beside her, "but how do you know me?"

He smiled in what she had always imagined to be a genuine fatherly manner. She smiled back.

"How could I not know you? You were like a daughter to Goldie."

Liz detected a subtle censure in his tone, but she was too concerned with his use of the past tense to give it much thought. "What do you mean *were*, Mr. Griffith?"

He met her gaze with compassion. "Goldie died, Liz, a month after you left for Europe."

He named the date, stunning Liz even further. Her lower lip began to tremble. "But she wasn't sick. Goldie never got sick! I talked to her on the phone just the day before."

"She simply died in her sleep, Liz."

Liz shook her head in denial. "She planned to leave for the West Coast that day. She was going to travel from San Diego to British Columbia because she'd never done it before. She was so excited about her trip, Mr. Griffith. She felt great. She said she even had a surprise for me when I got home."

Liz's big brown eyes grew moist, but she was too private a person to shed tears in front of a stranger. "She just can't be dead," she said in disbelief. "She's all I've got."

Griffith's pat on her shoulder felt more like a caress. Liz didn't like it.

"Someday you'll have a family of your own," he said, "and warm memories of Goldie to share with them, lessons to pass along. She would've expected you to mourn her for a time, but then she'd expect you to go forward, get on with your life."

Well and good for him to spout platitudes, Liz thought resentfully. Goldie hadn't been like a mother to him. Her eyes burned and her heart ached. She blinked several times to clear the tears. Her heart, however, did not know how to blink. It only knew how to beat and hurt, and right now it hurt worse than it ever had.

"I went all around the neighborhood this morning, and not one person even knew she was gone," Liz said in a daze. "Except the mailman. He's been watching the obituaries."

"There wasn't one. It seemed pointless to furnish an obituary to the newspaper when I knew that Goldie had virtually no friends."

Liz was only too aware of how true that was. "But there was at least a memorial service?"

"No."

"Why not?"

"Her family ordered a quick cremation."

Liz uttered a strangled tearful protest. Even with the lack of feelings between Liz and her own parents, she had done everything to ensure a traditional funeral service and burial for them. "How did her family find out about her death? They were never in contact." A sudden thought occurred to Liz. "Who found her?"

"Her daughter, Anna McGuinn. After that, everything was taken care of in less than twenty-four hours. The rest, as they say, is history."

Liz stared at him in shock. "Did you say McGuinn?"

"Yes."

"Jace McGuinn is living in Goldie's house."

"Yes, I know. He's Anna's son. His uncle Joe is a real-estate agent. He leased the house to Jace illegally, I might add, although I don't believe young McGuinn realizes that."

Liz didn't know much about legalities, but it didn't make sense that Jace couldn't lease the house. After all, he was Goldie's grandson.

"I've instituted legal proceedings on your behalf," Griffith went on.

"Why would you do that?"

A silver eyebrow shot up. "It's your house."

"Mine?"

"That and everything else belonging to Goldie." He shook his head. "I take it you are unaware that you are the beneficiary of the bulk of Goldie's estate."

Liz was not given to fainting, so she knew the little spots before her eyes did not mean she was going to lose consciousness. But that sudden roaring in her ears...she was positive she had misunderstood Chester B. Griffith's last remark.

"Excuse me?" she said politely.

He repeated himself. "Of course, she left the token dollar to each of her children, and ten thousand apiece to the grandchildren and great-grandchildren," he said matter-of-factly.

"And the house?" she asked. "Goldie left it to me?"

"That, and an estate valued at roughly four million dollars."

The spots grew bigger, the roaring louder.

Griffith shook his head in wonder. "You had no idea about all this, did you?"

Liz's head went back and forth very, very slowly.

Griffith muttered something unintelligible. "Goldie promised me she was going to tell you about the will, Liz. I had no idea you didn't know."

"Four million dollars?" she croaked. "What did she do? Rob a bank?"

Griffith leaned back and smiled. "The family always thought Giovanni was the brain in that marriage. Everyone was surprised when Goldie took over for him after his death."

"The family?"

He smiled the smile of a superior human being talking to a moron. "You know, the *family*."

Liz felt like a page had been ripped out of an especially gripping suspense novel she was reading. Her first instinct—to demand an explanation—was immediately overshadowed by the sudden suspicion forming in her mind. A suspicion she didn't very much like. The "family" he was talking about wasn't Goldie's offspring. "You mean, um, the underworld?"

He smiled again.

The numbness of her shock over Goldie's death was nudged by a nasty suspicion Liz wasn't up to examining too closely at the moment. Her anguish was already so deep it was actually a physical pain. She had to get away. Now.

Before she could compose a legitimate excuse, Griffith said, "You know, I think my favorite Goldie story was the one about the little Ming vase. She saw it in a museum in Paris and adored it. The next thing she knew, she owned it. It wasn't among the things I inventoried when we emptied out the house, though." His look became intent. "You know the piece I'm talking about?"

"I'm not sure I know what a Ming vase looks like," Liz admitted. "Goldie had lots of vases around. They were always full of flowers."

"You haven't seen any of them lately?"

"I haven't been around lately."

He offered her a benign smile. "It's very rare and worth a great deal of money, Liz. If you should happen to remember what she might have done with it, I'd like to know. As the executor of the estate, I have to account for it." He shook his head, affecting a rueful expression. "Damned if anyone could ever figure how Giovanni got that vase out of the museum."

Liz's determination to leave hadn't lessened while the attorney reminisced. "I really must be on my way, Mr. Griffith. I need to be alone for a while."

"Of course, Liz. I know this has all come as quite a shock to you."

"Quite," she agreed. What an understatement. Her thoughts were ricocheting off the walls of her mind like a spray of Mafia gunfire.

"If I can have your signature on the papers I've drawn up to serve Joe and Jace..."

"I don't want to sign anything right now," she protested. "I'll make an appointment in the next day or so."

Griffith looked about to argue, then snapped his mouth shut. "All right," he said. Much to her surprise, he added, "Jace McGuinn is a fine young man. He works hard. Had he channeled all that energy in another direction..." He shrugged, a wistful expression on his face.

"Was, I mean, uh, is he in Goldie's business?" she asked, then could have kicked herself for caring.

"No. The other uncle, Tony, was the only one with a propensity for following in his father's footsteps, but then Tony always did have his head in the clouds with his get-rich schemes."

Liz had a hundred unanswered questions before she mumbled her polite goodbye.

"Oh, Liz," Griffith called after her, "one more thing. I think you should know that if the heirs are performing true to form, you ought to be prepared for some ugliness."

Liz blinked at him, hoping to dispel this horrible living nightmare. "Ugliness," she repeated. "Great. I can hardly wait."

Liz was numb. Emotions she'd never known existed warred within her. Her grief was twofold: the death of Goldie and the emergence of a Goldie she didn't know. Even her parents, who had never made a secret of their lack of love for her, had never lied to her. Was it possible she had been fooled by the woman who'd been closer to her than her own mother?

She couldn't equate the Goldie Fabrizio she knew with the one Chester B. Griffith had described. She'd shared everything with Goldie. Had it all been a lie?

She didn't know what to believe. Eighteen years of love and caring couldn't be obliterated in one fell swoop. But if it was true, Goldie had bred liars, too. Her grandson was no different, no better. Jace McGuinn had known all along who Goldie was and what had happened to her, yet he'd played her for a fool.

She had a sudden violent urge to smack him right across his attractive chops.

By the time Liz reached her street, her anger had built to monumental proportions. When she stepped in a pile of something soft and squishy as she crossed the expanse of lawn between her house and Jace's, she was ready to commit murder. Not even the friendly greeting from the golden retriever, as it lapped its warm tongue across the back of her hand, soothed her temper.

No one answered when she banged her fist against the wood of Jace McGuinn's door. In her current state of mind, maybe it was just as well he *wasn't* home.

She sagged against the door frame, not sure whether to feel relief or rage. She ripped a deposit slip from her checkbook and scratched out a note. It took a minute of clever maneuvering to get it wedged between the weather stripping and the door.

Once cocooned in the privacy of her own home, she changed into jeans and T-shirt, poured herself a large glass of white wine and headed for the den. She plopped down in front of the TV, tormented with vague memories of the time before Goldie had come along and she'd spent too many childhood hours glued to the screen.

And here she was again, ready for some escapism, wondering if Goldie had gone to hell for committing the atrocities inherent with the underworld.

Liz gulped her wine and slipped further into the doldrums, her grief firmly buried beneath mounds and mounds of hurt and disbelief.

Was there ever really a friendship between the two of us? Liz wondered bleakly. *Was our relationship as superficial as borrowed sugar, or was it more complex, more concrete, more real?*

Liz rose and went to the entry hall where she lifted a small vase from the Shaker table. It was old and delicate and beautiful. How could she have carried sugar in it all those times and never realized it was a priceless antique?

She went back to the den and placed the vase on top of the TV, where it was in her immediate line of vision.

Armed with a box of tissues and the bottle of wine, Liz, who had never imbibed more than half a glass on special occasions, proceeded alternately to cry and drink herself into oblivion.

Three

It was dark when Jace got home. He shoved the key into the lock, then shouldered the door open and headed directly for the kitchen, where he deposited the grocery sacks in his arms on the tiled countertop.

He grabbed a cold beer from the refrigerator and went back to retrieve his keys and close the door. It was then that he noticed the small slip of paper on the floor. He took a draw from the frosty can before he bent to retrieve it. He read the note twice, took an extra long drink of his beer, then read it again. He was torn between laughter and a desire to strangle someone. Liz McAyeal sure had her nerve.

Crumpling the deposit slip in his fist, he shoved it into the pocket of his jeans. He drained the contents of the beer can, then proceeded to crumple it with equal fervor.

Little witch. Thought she could push him around, did she? Not likely. Until she messed with him, she didn't know what trouble was, he thought with a scowl.

Back in the kitchen, he withdrew the piece of paper from his pocket and smoothed it across the cool counter tiles. "Sorry to trouble you," it said, "but I would appreciate it if you would keep your dog and its leavings in your own yard."

Hell, he didn't even *have* a dog, so where did she get off blaming him for what someone else's pet had done in her yard?

Leavings? A rumble began deep in Jace's chest and finally the laugh burst forth. She sounded like some prim Victorian priss. *Leavings.* He collapsed into the nearest chair and continued to laugh until tears streamed down his cheeks.

Liz McAyeal was the only bright spot in this insanity his family had thrust upon him.

Damn, if she wasn't something.

Wednesday morning, the sun had the audacity to shine directly on Liz's face where she lay sprawled on the den floor.

On the perilous climb out of a drunken stupor, she pitched headfirst into the only hangover she'd ever experienced. Giant sledgehammers attacked her head from every angle and foul-tasting cotton balls had taken possession of her mouth. Stormy waves of nausea battered the walls of her stomach. In that moment, she vowed never to touch a drop of alcohol again.

To add insult to injury, the wine bottle had toppled over sometime during the night, spilling its meager contents on her formerly spotless rug.

Liz groaned, rolling away from both the sun's rays and the incriminating evidence. The sledgehammers beat harder with the sudden pounding at her door.

"Oh, Lord," she breathed as she tried to sit up. Bile crawled up her throat. Since she was about to die, anyway, she knew she should see who was there. Whoever it was could call the hearse.

The pounding intensified. Liz staggered to the door. She flipped the dead bolt and collapsed against the wall, holding her hand over her mouth.

The door opened. With glazed pleading eyes, she looked up at Jace McGuinn. For the moment, she forgot she hated his guts.

"Smells like a damned winery in here," he said cheerfully.

Liz's muffled response was unintelligible. Then her eyes widened.

Jace read the situation correctly and scooped her up in his powerful arms. Liz, in no condition to give directions, hung on tight. He took his best shot, choosing the downstairs hall, and located the small washroom tucked beneath the stairs.

Several minutes later, humiliated and embarrassed beyond belief, Liz lay exhausted against the cold porcelain commode while Jace McGuinn, that snake, applied a cold cloth to her face.

"If I'd known not responding to your note was going to make you suicidal, I'd have gone out and bought a pooper scooper," he joked.

"For a dog that size, you need a coal shovel!" Liz snapped.

He shook his head, a look of wonder creasing his face. "I thought drunks only saw elephants," he said. "You see dogs. Was it pink?"

Her eyes narrowed. "It's *your* dog," she hissed. "It messed in *my* yard. I want *you* to clean it up."

Jace shook his head, his expression and tone one of indulged patience. "I don't own a dog, honey."

"I saw it on your porch yesterday," she sputtered. "Twice. I can't believe you're denying it!"

"I haven't got a dog," he repeated.

"You're a liar!"

Some of his good humor evaporated. "I wouldn't be calling anyone names if I were you."

"Go away."

"C'mon, Lizzie, let's get you in the shower."

The man was apparently going deaf. "Don't call me Lizzie," she warned fiercely. "Never, ever call me that again. Goldie called me that."

"Okay, Lizzie. Up you go."

Deaf. And obtuse. *If I had a weapon, I'd use it on him,* she thought.

She was unable to offer more than a token protest as he lifted her once more and carried her up the stairs. Some instinct had him honing in on her bedroom. He deposited her in the adjoining bathroom, chuckled when she told him where he could put his offer to help her undress and left her to go downstairs and put on a pot of coffee.

Feeling half-human again after fifteen minutes in the shower, Liz dressed and made her way down to the kitchen where Jace had apparently appointed himself head chef.

She watched him for a moment, towering over a pan at the stove, scrambling eggs.

"I'm not hungry," she said.

"I am."

"By all means, then, make yourself at home."

He grinned over his broad shoulder at her. "Thanks. Coffee's done."

Liz looked around for something to throw at him.

She crossed to the coffeepot, Jace hot on her tail. "Here's some aspirin," he said, his palm extended.

Liz took the tablets he proffered, and the glass of water, with a resentful thanks. She climbed up on a stool at the breakfast bar and watched sullenly as he devoured four eggs, three pieces of toast and a banana.

"Your parents must have had tremendous grocery bills," she muttered.

"Still do," he said. "Five of us kids. Two still at home."

"Five?" she asked, intrigued in spite of herself. Coming from a one-child family, where even one had been too many, five sounded like heaven. She really wanted to know more about his family, but right now she was irked with him for having witnessed the absolute lowest point of her life. And he had lied to her. She wanted revenge more than she wanted to know about his family.

"What's your occupation, McGuinn? I bet you're a real piranha in the business world."

He looked her straight in the eye, evidently trying to gauge her mood. "I'm a financial adviser, Lizzie. Careful sound investments for myself and for my clients. I do okay at it."

His casual acceptance of what she guessed to be an understatement of his success riled her even further. "You get rich off other people's money?" she goaded.

He considered her a moment, then delivered his salvo in an ominously soft tone. "At least I come by their money honestly."

His implication took a moment to sink in. "What's that supposed to mean?"

"Nothing."

"You think I befriended your grandmother for her money?"

"I guess that means you know who I am."

"Obviously."

"Yeah," he said, a wry twist lifting the corner of his mouth. "Obviously."

They stared each other down. The pounding at Liz's temples hindered her thought processes. Still, she noticed something she hadn't the day before.

Jace McGuinn had a lot of his grandmother in him. No wonder certain mannerisms and speech patterns of his seemed so familiar. And those blue blue eyes.

She worked hard at keeping her tears at bay. "What's not so obvious is why you didn't tell me about Goldie. Why did you hide her death from me?"

"I didn't know."

"Liar!"

His eyes chilled. "I don't lie, Lizzie."

"And you think I do?"

He studied her face intently for a moment. "I don't know."

Liz could have pursued that, but she had a more pressing issue on her mind. "How could you not know she was dead?"

Jace slammed the fingers of one hand through his hair and laughed. It wasn't a sound of humor. "I didn't even know I had a grandmother until yesterday afternoon."

"Oh, please!"

"I'm telling you, I didn't. I thought she died years ago."

"Your family told you she was dead?" Liz couldn't keep the disbelief from her tone.

"Dammit, Lizzie, I was just a kid. How was I supposed to know the difference when I'd never even met her?"

"Your mother and your uncles are a real piece of work, McGuinn."

"Don't start. From what I hear, you aren't exactly the girl next door."

All color drained from her face. She tried unsuccessfully to keep the hurt from her expression and her voice. "It's time for you to leave."

His face creased with regret. "Liz—"

"Now!"

"Dammit, Liz. I'm sorry."

"'Sorry' doesn't cut it," she said flatly. "I didn't know Goldie had money or that she'd named me in her will."

"Yeah, I'll just bet."

His renewed cynicism cut through Liz with all the finesse of a dull razor. Her voice took on a bitter edge. "You're right, I'm not the girl next door, and I didn't grow up in a perfect little house mommied by June Cleaver, but I got something better with Goldie."

"A hefty bank account is a pretty cold substitute."

"I'm not talking about money, McGuinn. I'm talking about love."

She marched out of the kitchen, her shoulders squared despite the hurt, anger and grief smothering her. "For your information, I told the attorney I would talk to him in a couple of days about your occupancy of the house."

"What the hell?" Jace was on her heels in a flash. He grabbed her arm and whirled her around. "What do you mean by that? I have a lease agreement."

"Goldie left the house to me," Liz said, ignoring the pain of his fingers digging into the tender flesh of her arm. "Your uncle had no right to lease it. To you or anybody. You'll both be damned lucky if I don't bring criminal charges against you." He jerked back as if he'd just touched hot lava.

"Get out, McGuinn."

Liz was halfway up the stairs when she heard him open the door and slam it behind him.

She was totally, utterly weary. Everywhere she looked, deceit smacked her in the face. Everywhere she turned, she stepped on another lie. She had loved and trusted Goldie for eighteen years, and now she was faced with the possibility that everything about her best friend and mentor had been a lie. Every damned thing!

Liz crawled into bed.

She slept the clock around, but her sleep wasn't sound. Jace McGuinn's nonexistent dog spent most of the day barking at the birds and the night baying at the moon.

By the time Liz awoke on Friday morning, she had a plan.

Before she left she removed the vase from the TV set and carried it back out to the Shaker table. As she cradled it carefully between her palms, she decided that, Ming or not, she wanted to keep this object she would always think of as the sugar cup. With luck, it wouldn't remind her of her stupidity and gullibility, but of her good times with Goldie. Its monetary value was unimportant.

She then headed straight for the public library, to the room where she could peruse old newspapers and magazines for accounts of the "family's" involvement in the community, and more specifically, about Giovanni Fabrizio.

Hours later, Liz rubbed at her eyes. Staring at microfiche had made them ache and burn. She looked at the pile of photocopies and books beside her and decided she'd had enough for one day. As it was, her weekend would be packed with consuming information about organized crime.

Not five minutes after she deposited her load on the dining-room table, there was a tapping, then a pounding on her door. Jace McGuinn, Liz was certain. She ignored the summons, unplugged the phones and returned to the haven of her bed. Rude or not, she didn't want to talk to him or anyone else.

Several hours later, she awoke from a restless slumber to the annoying sound of a barking dog. Again. After a few minutes, she gave up trying to sleep, since she wasn't anxious to fall back into the same dream patterns, and stomped over to the window. The golden retriever her new neighbor denied owning straddled the property line, barking its fool head off.

Liz glanced at the clock. It was just past nine. Jace McGuinn's lights were on, and unless he had his music or TV blaring, there was no way he couldn't hear that dog. She reached for the phone, then realized she didn't know his number. Not one to let a minor inconvenience stop her, she dialed directory assistance. No listing.

She thought about climbing back into bed with cotton shoved in her ears, but the noise was atrocious. Instead, she climbed into a pair of jeans and a sweatshirt and stormed barefoot over to his house. She knocked, then put her ear to the wood and listened. Silence. Except for the gentle pant of the dog, which had followed her to the porch.

Liz turned a look of disgust on the animal. "You mangy fur ball," she muttered. "How am I supposed to prove you were barking when you're sitting there with your tongue hanging out, wagging your tail?" Without even thinking about it, she reached out and scratched behind the creature's ears. "Dumb dog," she went on absently. "You're almost as dumb as your master."

Liz knocked again, wondering why Jace hadn't installed a doorbell or a knocker, when he seemed the sort who liked modern conveniences. A moment later, almost at the same instant she heard him barreling down the stairs, the dog licked her hand, then took off running toward the backyard.

The door flew open and Liz found herself tongue-tied. Jace McGuinn was the most undeniably *male* man she'd ever met. She'd thought so every time she'd seen him, and now was no different. He had on tiny little sweat shorts and a half-T-shirt that gave her more to look at than was good for her libido. She swallowed over the sudden lump in her throat and forced herself to speak. "It's about the dog," she began. "His barking woke me up."

With the light behind him, Liz couldn't read his expression accurately, but the way his head dipped, it didn't take a genius to figure out that he was looking her over. Her body temperature rose just thinking about it. "I told you I don't have a dog, Lizzie."

"Then who does that golden retriever belong to?" she persisted.

"I haven't seen any golden retriever."

Liz was getting a little tired of his game. "Well, I have. Either on your porch or in my yard barking or doing you-know-what." He crossed his arms over his chest and she couldn't prevent her eyes being drawn to the taut flat belly exposed beneath the lower edge of his shirt.

Jace nodded with amused patience. "Ah, yes. Leaving its leavings."

Liz felt like kicking him.

"And where is this dog now?" he drawled.

"It just ran around behind the house."

Jace flipped on the porch light, nearly blinding her. "Let's go see."

Liz was willing. She turned and preceded him down the steps, resisting the urge to turn around and tell him to take his eyes off her backside.

"Don't step in anything," he warned, his long strides carrying him past her as they rounded the corner of the house.

"The dog messes in my yard, not yours."

"There're other things besides that on the ground. I haven't put any slug bait out yet."

After that, Liz watched where she put her feet on the flagstone walkway.

Of course, there was no dog. Neither of them needed a flashlight to see that. The moon was full—the dog *had* been baying at it for the past three nights—but no matter how she coaxed, the animal didn't appear from the shadows.

"I told you I don't have a dog," Jace said, heading for the French doors at the back of the house.

"I tell you I've seen it."

"Lizzie—"

His mollifying tone infuriated her. "I'm going to call animal control next time."

"Go ahead," he said. "I'm telling you the dog's not mine." He leaned against the house, his eyes skimming her briefly before he said, "Look, why don't you come in for a cup of coffee?"

There was a suggestiveness about the invitation and the accompanying visual caress that left certain parts of Liz's body heated up. "Um, some other time. I think I left the stove on."

She turned, only to be stopped by Jace's hand on her arm. "I've been able to get a few things straightened out with my family, Lizzie."

His features tightened momentarily with an emotion Liz recognized as pain. "That's between you and them," she said. "It's none of my business."

"They made it your business when they talked me into moving into this house."

Liz couldn't dispute that, but she also wasn't ready to discuss it. Not when she was feeling protective of him, not when she was wondering what that hand would feel like under her sweatshirt.

Disgusted with her hot-blooded thoughts, she pulled away and quickly detoured back to the flagstone. She grimaced when she felt something slimy and sticky beneath her foot, but she let neither that, nor Jace calling out to her, delay her hasty retreat home.

The dog met her halfway across the yard. "Now, how did I know you'd show up?" Liz asked. She stopped for a moment, looking down at the animal, examining it for tags. "Since you don't belong to him and you don't appear to belong to anyone else, either, how would you like to belong to me?"

The dog yipped excitedly.

"I thought that's what you'd say," she returned dryly. "C'mon." The dog followed obediently at her side. Liz stopped at the hose to rinse off her foot. "I wonder what your name is," she said at the door. "Goldie always said if she had a golden retriever she was going to call it Daisy." She opened the door and the dog stepped inside. "I hate to be rude," she went on, "but are you a boy or a girl?"

The dog promptly rolled over for a belly rub and Liz had her question answered. "Daisy it is, then." Daisy jumped up on all fours and put her head on Liz's knee. "Welcome to the land of insanity, lies and fantasy, Daisy."

The dog whined.

Liz stood and trooped upstairs to get her shoes. "I'm going out to get you some food," she said several minutes later.

With keys in hand, she walked right by Daisy, never noticing that the dog sat on her haunches, head cocked, staring intently at the sugar cup.

Four

Even with Daisy in the house, Liz felt lonely. The dog was affectionate and friendly, but Liz was still grieving for Goldie. She wanted her friend back.

When Liz fell into bed each night, the cacophony in her mind kept immediate oblivion at bay. Only after hours of endless thinking and tossing did sleep claim her.

During the day she ruminated endlessly over how best to make things right for the people whose lives Goldie had ruined. *I didn't want your millions of dollars or your house or your precious Ming vase,* her mind screamed in silent rage time and time again. *I wanted* you, *Goldie, your love! Your truth, dammit, not your lies.*

And, Goldie, you should see your grandson. He's the image of you, right down to the way he eats chocolate-chip cookies and lies through his teeth. The worst of it is, I could fall for him, Goldie.

After five days of vacillating between feeling sorry for herself and wishing for a way to vent her anger, she'd had enough. She'd spent hours poring over old newspaper clippings and reading magazine articles. She could recite most of what she'd read backward.

Chester B. Griffith called to get her decision on legal action regarding Goldie's house, but she hadn't reached one. He reminded her that Goldie had cleverly amassed a fortune. Liz needed to start thinking about investments of her own. He had some ideas.

Fortunes, investments. None of it altered the fact that Goldie had lied to her, not outright, of course, but by omission. And now Liz had to get on with her life knowing that. Forget the betrayal. Learn to live with it. She'd done it before, she'd do it again. "Right, Daisy?" she asked the dog.

Armed with a plastic pan full of cleaning supplies, Liz headed for the upstairs bathroom. Daisy trailed after her.

Liz spent the entire day scrubbing her house from top to bottom. She cleaned everything that needed cleaning, and most of what didn't. Finally at five o'clock she took a break. She was about to pour herself a tall glass of iced tea when the doorbell chimed.

She quickly straightened her clothes and batted at the straggling wisps of hair that had escaped her ponytail.

With Daisy at her side, she went to the door. The man standing there was no one she knew.

"Elizabeth Anne McAyeal?" he asked.

Liz nodded.

"Here you go," he said cheerfully, handing her a white envelope. He tipped his hat to her, spun on his heel and walked away whistling.

Liz stared at the envelope, ignoring Daisy's whine of concern. The dog nudged her bare leg with a wet nose. "I have a bad feeling about this, girl."

Daisy yipped.

Liz closed the door and went back to the kitchen. Once the envelope was open, her fears were confirmed. The ugliness had begun. She didn't know whether to scream with frustration, laugh hysterically or cry.

"Tony, Joe and Anna want it all," she said to Daisy. "I wonder what they'll do when they find out there's not going to be anything left to have."

* * *

Liz arose at seven and did something she hadn't done since her thirteenth summer. She turned on Saturday-morning cartoons.

Muppet Babies squealed at her. Ghostbusters attempted to suck her into their trap. She couldn't say which was more absurd—the cartoons or the commercials.

Goldie had taken her away from all this. Unless she watched "Evening at the Pops" or a special documentary, Liz rarely sat in front of the television. Sometimes she wondered why she even owned one at all.

Now she had to contend with a stupid lawsuit on top of everything else. Liz pointed the remote control at the TV and flipped the channels as she sipped at her coffee. Daisy lay at her feet, her doggie eyebrows bouncing up and down as she watched the activity on the screen.

Liz finished her coffee and shut off the set. "Let's go see Jace McGuinn, girl. I want to hear what he has to say about this lawsuit."

Daisy raised her head, yawned, then dropped it back against her paws and closed her eyes.

"I guess that means you aren't going."

Already asleep, Daisy twitched.

Liz didn't notice the cars at the curb when she marched over to Jace McGuinn's house—*her* house—for some answers. She was too busy thinking about whether or not she trusted him. He was either the best actor in the world, or he'd been telling the truth about not knowing he was living in the house that had belonged to his grandmother for almost twenty years.

The memory of the signatures on the lawsuit kept screaming at her. She wanted to know why one of them wasn't Jace's. She wanted some truth, but she also wanted to mend some fences, if she'd been wrong about more than the dog.

She wanted to be fair.

In one hand she held a basket of freshly baked chocolate-chip cookies. In the other, she clutched a bouquet of Shasta daisies from her yard.

"Hi," Jace said when he pulled open the door. She was certain she detected a genuine warmth in the greeting.

"Hi," she said. "I came to apologize."

He glanced down at her offerings, then back at her, smiling. His eyes sparkled with something more than glad-to-see-you. Liz shook her head to dispel the notion. No, it couldn't be that. She'd been at cross-purposes, as well as acting rude and testy, since the first moment they'd met. That couldn't be desire she read in his eyes.

"Come on in, Lizzie. I think I have a little apologizing of my own to do." He paused. "You're just in time to meet some of my family."

Liz's smile faltered. She tried to peek around him, but his form filled the doorway. "Aside from saying I'm sorry, I came over to talk to you about the papers I was served yesterday," she admitted, "but I don't think it would be a good idea if any of the plaintiffs are here."

Jace raised a dark eyebrow and grinned. "Oh, honey, I like it when you talk legal."

Liz couldn't help herself. She grinned back. "You should hear me when I talk medical," she confided.

Jace gave a hoot of laughter.

"Hey, Jace, what's so funny? Who're you hiding at the door?"

Liz didn't recognize the voice, but as soon as the older man appeared behind Jace, equaling him in size and stature, she knew it must be either Tony or Joe. The family resemblance was remarkable. Though older, Jace's uncle was as attractive and fit as most men half his age.

"This is my uncle Tony, Lizzie. You may remember him from his signature."

Tony offered his hand and a friendly smile, but frowned at Jace's choice of words.

Liz took the older man's hand. "He means I'm your adversary, Tony. The one you're suing for Goldie's estate."

Tony said something in Italian, pulling his hand back as if Liz had scalded him. *"You're* Elizabeth?"

Swearing in Italian sounded interesting, she decided, and made a note to buy an Italian dictionary. "One and the same."

"But . . ." Helpless, Tony looked at Jace.

His nephew leaned against the doorjamb. "She doesn't look like a money-grubbing little bitch, does she?"

Tony colored with indignation. "Watch your mouth, Jason McGuinn, or I'll smack you."

Jace shrugged and looked at Liz, his eyes full of devilment. "You can see how tough he is."

A humorous rejoinder sprang to her lips, but she caught it just in time. This was a serious matter. Jace's uncles and his mother were suing her for everything Goldie was worth. "I'll come back another time."

Jace grabbed her elbow, propelling her forward. "This is a good time right now. The family's gathered round, the cookies smell fresh, and the daisies haven't started to droop. Mom and Joe are in the kitchen. Let's join them."

A perverse little demon inside Liz wanted to stay, wanted to make these people as uncomfortable and angry as they made her. "All right."

Still holding the cookies and flowers, Liz's eyes swept the kitchen from where she and Jace stood beneath the archway. Joe-the-real-estate-agent was a younger version of Tony, and Anna was a startling Sophia Loren-type beauty. Sweet and loving and deceitful as she had been, Goldie had been a petite, second-generation American of English parentage, with a plain-Jane face but a glorious head of golden hair that had made men look twice. All of Goldie's children resembled the picture Liz had once seen of Giovanni Fabrizio. She wondered if, like Jace, any of the other grandchildren had Goldie's blue eyes.

Despite the predicament she suddenly found herself in, Liz recalled the way Jace McGuinn had been looking at her a few minutes earlier with those eyes of his. She was no raving beauty, but she certainly wasn't unattractive. A delicious shiver skittered down her spine, and it was a moment before she realized Jace's uncles and mother were all talking to her at once.

"Excuse me?" she said politely.

Anna McGuinn extended her hand, a warm smile on her face. Liz took it warily.

"Jason's told me quite a lot about you, Elizabeth. It's nice to meet you," Anna said.

"It's Liz," Liz corrected automatically, and couldn't resist adding, "I only go by Elizabeth for legal purposes."

Anna had the good grace to blush.

"I'm Joe," said Jace's youngest uncle, also offering his hand.

Liz almost said, "Nice to meet you," but she wasn't sure it *was* nice, so she held her tongue and just shook his hand.

"Liz brought cookies," Jace said. "The coffee should be done by now." Implicit in his words were instructions to sit down, which his mother and uncles did without a word.

Liz followed him to the coffeemaker. "Can I help?"

Jace smiled at her over his shoulder. "Cream's in the fridge."

Grateful for something to do, Liz moved to the refrigerator.

"Well," Jace said a few moments later, "isn't this cozy? The plaintiffs and the defendant all at the same table." He took two cookies from the basket and bit into one, ignoring the uncomfortable silence around the table. "So, who's going first?"

"First?" Anna asked, sipping nervously from her cup.

"Yeah, you know. Who's going to tell Lizzie she should give up Goldie's estate and why?"

Joe choked on his coffee.

"You got a smart mouth, Jace," Tony blustered. "Just like your grandmother."

Jace leaned back in his chair, a spark of interest in his eyes. "Oh, yeah?" He glanced at Joe and his mother, then back at Tony. "I thought none of us was like her. I thought she was a mean old lady, out for the almighty buck, regardless of who she stepped on."

Anna sucked in a breath and Liz noticed her eyes were glistening with unshed tears. "Don't talk about Mama that way, Jace."

"*You* did," Jace pointed out with a gentleness that belied the steel behind his words.

"We all did," Tony said, coming to his sister's defense. Joe remained silent. "We thought she *was* a mean old lady. That's why we said it."

Liz looked at each of them in turn. They seemed to have forgotten she was there. "She wasn't mean," she said softly, and wondered exactly when she had forgiven Goldie for deceiving her. There was strength in years of loving and being loved. "She was the kindest, most loving person I've ever known."

Shocked silence greeted her declaration, then Jace's uncles and his mother burst into excited rebuttal. Liz tried to speak without success, and it was finally Jace's roar of "Quiet!" that stilled them.

"You're going to make Liz think you're all crazy," he said easily.

She didn't *think* it, Liz thought.

"You don't know what you're talking about, Elizabeth," Tony cut in. "Mama never had time to spend on loving anybody."

Anna nodded in agreement as Joe said, "She never took an interest in anything we did."

"She did, only you didn't know it," Liz said, even as another thought occurred to her. "Is that why you thought it would be okay to lease this house to Jace? Some sort of revenge? Repayment?"

Tony blustered, ready to defend his brother's actions, but Joe put up his hand to stave him off. "Mama wanted Jace to have this house."

"How do you know that?"

"I told her what he was looking for..." He trailed off, helpless with his inability to justify his wrong.

Jace's face went still. "You told my grandmother I wanted this house?"

Joe looked so miserable Liz almost felt sorry for him. "No," he said, "but I planned to. I just *knew* it was what you were looking for. I didn't know Mama gave everything to the—to Liz. I figured once probate was over, you could just buy it."

Liz gave Jace points for not asking his uncle where the money for the monthly lease had been going. "If Goldie had known you wanted this house, she wouldn't have given it to me," she told him.

Liz could tell by the emotion clouding his eyes that Jace wanted to believe her. He wanted to very much. "You must have seen a different side of her, Lizzie."

"I still didn't know everything," she said, unable to keep the trace of bitterness from her voice.

Jace reached for her hand. "No one really knew what my grandmother was like."

"All of you should have known. Families are supposed to know about each other." Liz tossed her head impatiently. "*I* should have known! Her attorney knew. He thought *I* knew. He'd made Goldie promise to tell me everything when she had her will drawn up."

Tony sneered. "And you would have refused to be the beneficiary, right?"

Liz felt Jace's fingers tighten around hers. She looked Tony directly in the eye. "You don't know me, so I don't expect you to believe this, but you're right. I would've told her not to name me in the will. I don't need the money."

Once again, Tony swore eloquently in Italian and would have said more if Anna hadn't restrained him with a quelling look.

Liz didn't feel any compulsion to make Tony, or even Anna or Joe, who seemed somehow sympathetic, understand how it was between her and Goldie, but for some reason, it was important that Jace know.

Liz had suffered long years of antipathetic captivity in a home where the slightest show of affection was discouraged, even forbidden. She used to wonder endlessly why her parents had conceived and borne a child. They had provided every material thing she needed, and more that she'd neither wanted nor asked for, yet they had withheld the one thing that was most important to her. Their love.

Liz gave up trying to have a normal relationship with her parents the way other kids had. She never went home with friends and never invited them to her house. Safety came in solitude. She kept to herself, got all her homework done right on time and spent a lot of time watching television. Goldie had turned the shy little brown-haired, brown-eyed girl called Elizabeth into a person named Liz, who was confident, outgoing and friendly.

"I'll never forget when Goldie moved in next door," she began. "It was a beautiful spring day. The crocuses were already up and the tulips were ready to bloom." Even though she was saying this for Jace, Liz couldn't look at him. She kept her gaze trained on the cup in front of her. "Every afternoon, on my way home from school, I'd see Goldie working the earth. She was so diligent about it that she eventually had the yard looking like a lush fantasy garden." She glanced at Jace then. He was staring at her with rapt attention.

"At first, all we did was say hello to each other. She was a lot friendlier about it than I was, but it didn't take long for us to become fast friends. After a while I found myself spending more time here than at home."

She searched each of their expressions. In Tony's she saw disbelief, in Joe's, uncertainty. In Anna's there was compassion and in Jace's, longing. "I can't tell you how it was not to have to spend all those long lonesome hours doing homework or hidden away in that dreary room my parents called a den, in front of the TV. They liked it best when they never knew I was in the house. At Goldie's I could run and play, or cry, or laugh—and it was okay."

"You poor thing," Anna murmured.

"I'm not looking for sympathy," Liz said not unkindly.

Goldie had easily and naturally become more important to her than her own parents. She lived through the trauma of Liz's first menstrual period, her first boyfriend, her first lover. She had wept for joy at Liz's accomplishments and given her unflagging encouragement when she was down.

"Goldie said we were kindred spirits," Liz said, remembering Jace had said the same thing, though for different reasons. "We were both lonely, and we helped each other ease that loneliness. She helped me grow into the person I am today." Liz choked on those last words. Maybe she *hadn't* completely forgiven Goldie for the lies. "She did all that, yet she ruined so many lives..."

Suddenly tears streamed down her cheeks. "I'm sorry!" she cried and, before anyone could stop her, pushed away from the table. She ran for the door and the safety of her own home.

"Poor kid," Joe said, shaking his head.

"Poor kid, my ass," Tony scoffed. "She's got that dramatic streak in her, just like Mama. Hell, Mama probably taught her how to cultivate it."

"I don't understand," Anna said, her own voice clogged with tears. "How could Mama turn away from all of us and do so much for someone who wasn't even her own flesh and blood?"

"That's a good question," Jace said, his tone cold, his expression speculative. "Why do I get the feeling you three know the answer?"

Five

The TV was on when Liz walked into the house.

At first she didn't notice it. She was crying. She was angry. She'd just bared her soul in front of Jace's relatives, and for what? She thought she owed them? She thought they deserved to know, to understand, why Goldie had left her a fortune?

Why did she feel guilty? Why had she apologized? They were only interested in Goldie's money. Not in Goldie. Not in the innocent lives she'd destroyed.

Daisy nuzzled Liz's hand where it rested on the arm of the chair. "I think I made a fool of myself, girl."

The dog woofed sympathetically. It was then that Liz realized the television was on. "I thought I switched that off before I left," she said. Her gaze swung from the toy commercial to Daisy. "Did you learn to turn the TV on while I was gone?" she asked with teasing suspicion.

Daisy sat down on her haunches and cocked her head.

Liz swiped at her tears and offered her new pet a lopsided grin. "Guess not, huh? Pretty stupid question." She reached for the remote control.

After dinner, Liz curled up in the corner of the sofa with a book in hand and a cup of tea beside her. "Evening at the Pops" was on, but she'd had more than enough television for one day. Another type of escapism was in order.

She hadn't been reading more than a few minutes when the doorbell sounded. Unless she was being served with a second lawsuit, Liz had a pretty good idea who was there.

She pulled open the door to find Jace McGuinn with his hand planted on the jamb, his big body filling the doorway. Liz said nothing.

"I would have been over sooner," Jace said, "but I had some thinking to do."

"Did it hurt?"

"Ooh, Lizzie, you do know how to maim. Mind if I come in?"

Without waiting for her response, Jace eased by her. Liz jumped back, but not soon enough to avoid his body brushing against hers in all the right places. Little shock waves coursed through her. Being attracted to him wasn't on the agenda, she reminded herself silently. She was thirty years old, dammit. She ought to be able to curb her biological urges.

"What do you want?"

Jace cocked an eyebrow at her.

Liz realized she was being hostile, but it was a defense mechanism that came automatically when Goldie's grandson was near. "I'm sorry," she said, running a hand through the long loose strands of her hair.

Jace's eyes followed the movement, then dropped lower to where her T-shirt pulled taut over her breasts. Liz cursed whatever demon had prompted her to go without a bra after her shower.

By the time he met her eyes again, Liz was feeling hot and flushed and her pulse was hammering erratically. He might as well have had his hands on her bare skin. The effect was the same.

Jace didn't seem to be faring much better. The pulse beat in his neck was accelerated and his words came out in a gruff whisper. "I came over to tell you *I'm* sorry."

He had that look in his eyes again. Desire curled through her with an alarming intensity. "For what? Your family?"

"Yes," he said, surprising her.

"Don't. I learned a long time ago, if you feel you have to apologize for your family, you'll spend all your time doing that and you'll get nothing else accomplished."

His expression softened. "Your folks really did a number on you, didn't they, Lizzie?"

Her breath caught in her throat.

"I can't begin to imagine what that was like," Jace said. "Mom and Dad loved all of us kids so much that sometimes it was embarrassing."

"You were lucky."

"I know that now, but when I was a kid, it was a burden." He took a step closer and raised his hand to her face. He ran the pad of his thumb over her lips. "I'm glad my grandmother was there for you, Lizzie."

Liz, trembling under his touch, lowered her lashes so he couldn't read the emotion churning in her. "How can you be glad, when she wasn't there for you?"

"I'm not sure," he admitted. "But I know it wouldn't have been right if you'd grown up without her."

Slowly Liz looked up at him, her heart and her desire in her eyes. She could feel the heat of him, though several inches separated their bodies.

"Lizzie..."

"What?" she whispered, unconsciously leaning forward.

"I want to make love to you," Jace murmured hoarsely.

Liz wasn't sure whether to be incensed or excited by his audacity. The thundering pulse surging through her head, the tingling in strategic places, assured her his statement had been well-received by her baser feminine core.

"I—" Before she could complete the sentence, Jace hauled her up against the hard length of his body, settling his mouth on hers with possessive fierceness.

Liz was lost in a maelstrom of emotions. She was hot and cold. She was blinded with a sudden passion that left her weak-kneed and buzzing in certain bodily regions that hadn't been alive for a long time, if ever.

Jace's tongue darted in and out of her mouth. Hers dueled back, and he must have taken that for the invitation it was. Before she knew it, the rough pads of his fingers were caressing her bare breasts beneath the T-shirt and his other hand was cupping her derriere beneath her shorts, bringing her firmly against the positive proof of his desire for her. His touch was better than anything her imagination had conjured up.

He tore his mouth from hers, and his lips went on a quest down her throat and neck, halting at a place below her ear she never would have guessed was a center of sensitivity. His breath fanned hot and quick against her skin.

Liz was not, by nature, impulsive. She never in a million years would have believed she would succumb to Jace's—or anyone's—lovemaking on the floor of her living room, but that was exactly what she found herself doing.

Her clothes had disappeared and Jace's seemed to be going at an astonishing rate. She was too busy enjoying what he was doing to her body—and what he was letting her do to his—to care that she barely knew him. Despite that, what they were doing seemed right. Every touch was such exquisite pleasure she was sure she was going to die from it.

Vaguely, she heard Jace mutter about inconvenient packaging. It occurred to her to be thankful that at least one of them had thought to take precautions.

In that moment of lucidity, it also occurred to Liz to wonder exactly what she was doing. But then Jace eased himself between her thighs and entered her with one swift deep stroke and she no longer cared about anything but sensation.

"I didn't come over here for this," Jace said sometime later.

They had moved upstairs to Liz's bed. Curled against his chest, her hand roaming over the hair-roughened surface, she tilted her head to look at him. "You didn't?"

He shook his head. "I've been thinking about it since the first time I saw you, but I didn't come over primarily to make love to you tonight."

"So you always travel with a rubber in your pocket?" she asked bluntly.

Jace stilled. "I said it wasn't the primary reason, Lizzie. I never said it wasn't a secondary reason."

Liz tweaked one of his nipples, too sated to take offense. "You're ramming your foot farther into your mouth, McGuinn. A woman likes to think she's the number-one priority of the man she—" She broke off, appalled at what she'd almost said. She'd known Jace McGuinn for little more than a week. She didn't feel *anything* for him. Nothing. *Nada.*

"The man she what, Lizzie?"

"She sleeps with," Liz improvised.

Jace sighed deeply, but didn't challenge her. Instead, he settled back and slid his hands beneath his head. "Mom and Tony and Joe decided that what you told them about my grandmother jibes with how they remember her when they were growing up. They say it wasn't until they were all adults that she cut them out of her life, but none of them has a clue why."

Liz tensed against Jace's chest. "Wait a minute! I was always under the impression that *they* were the ones who did the cutting."

"No way. Tony's wife was pregnant with my oldest cousin when the split came. Molly would have been the first grandchild, but my grandmother told Tony in no uncertain terms that she never wanted to see him—or any of us—again."

"I can't believe that," Liz said. "It doesn't sound like Goldie at all. She loved children. She was sad all the time because she never got to see her children or grandchildren.'' She raised herself up on her forearms, peering intently into Jace's eyes. "When she found out about her first great-grandchild, she sat down and wept.''

A shudder rippled through Jace. "We all lost so much.''

"You had her love, Jace. You just didn't know it.''

He pulled his hands from behind his head and crushed Liz against him in a powerful embrace. "Then why didn't she try and see us?''

Liz's heart broke at his longing and anguish. "I don't know.'' But she had an idea how they could find out.

Jace was still sleeping when Liz awoke the next morning. It was the first time a man had ever spent the night in her bed, and it felt right. He was a magnificent lover, but more than that, they connected on other levels. Each talked and the other listened. She *felt* what Jace was saying, just as she was sure he *felt* what she was saying. Without stopping to analyze things too deeply, she knew that what they had was special.

As Liz eased out of bed and into a cotton nightie she pulled from the drawer, she mentally examined the contents of her cupboards and refrigerator.

At the bottom of the stairs, she paused and looked at the sugar cup. She'd never pointed it out to Jace or even mentioned it to him. Did she dare? They had skirted around the issue of the lawsuit during the night, so she really had no idea how he felt about it. Did he support his family? Was blood really thicker than water? After all, he'd only known Liz for a short time. Intimacy such as they shared for the past eight or nine hours hardly qualified as the type of relationship that instilled loyalty.

Liz picked up the Ming and studied it, as if it could tell her something about its history under Goldie's roof. With a sigh, she replaced it and headed for the kitchen.

Halfway through the dining room, where she had the books and clippings from the library spread out over the table, she stopped and turned to study the scene.

Not quite sure what was wrong, she approached the table. Normally, she was not the most organized person, but because she had brought home so much material from the library, then collected even more from the bookstore, she had tried to put some order to the mess cluttering the tabletop.

That current order, to her recollection, was not the same order she had left in the room two nights before.

An uneasy prickle caused goose bumps on her arms. For some reason she didn't examine too carefully, she felt compelled to inspect every room of the big old house.

Nothing else had been disturbed anywhere. Jace was still sprawled on his stomach, the sheet riding low on his firm buttocks. Liz couldn't help the purely feminine tremble of appreciation that coursed through her. Despite that attraction, she had to wonder if he had gone through the house while she slept.

Somehow the idea seemed ludicrous, but if not Jace, then who?

Pensively ticking off the possibilities as she headed back for the kitchen, Liz came up with four suspects.

Since dogs didn't read, that left only three. All of them were related to the man in her bed.

Liz was putting the finishing touches on a fruit plate when Jace came up behind her. He slid his powerful arms beneath her breasts and pulled her backside up against his front side, where he was swollen with desire.

"Ever consider cooking in the buff?" he growled against her ear.

All rational thought fled her mind. She wiggled against him in unconscious seduction. "Not until this moment."

Jace's hands teased at her breasts for a moment, then reached down and pulled her nightie up over her head with a slow tantalizing movement that left her breathless.

"Can breakfast wait?" he asked as he turned her and began to lavish the fullness of her suddenly heavy breasts with his tongue.

"Y. . ." She cleared her throat and tried again. "Yes."

"Good," he growled, and before she knew what was happening, Jace had scooped her up in his arms and carried her back upstairs to bed.

Much later, their passion temporarily satisfied, Liz noted in a lazy content voice, "I thought women only got carted up the stairs in books."

Jace's chest rumbled with his chuckle. "I thought so, too. You make me do things I've never done before, Lizzie."

It was a perfect opportunity. "Did you wake during the night and look through the books and newspaper clippings in the dining room?"

"Huh?"

"I have some reference materials on the table in the dining room. Did you go through them last night?"

"I was busy all night, honey, and when I wasn't, I was sleeping, trying to get my strength back."

Liz couldn't believe it when she felt herself blush, but she did believe him. Her silence stretched so long Jace pulled back, then took her chin between his fingers and tilted her head to see her expression better. "Want to tell me what's going on?"

Feeling foolish for worrying about something that was probably the result of her own memory lapse, Liz shrugged. She *had* been under a great deal of strain lately. "I just thought things had been disturbed, but I'm probably not remembering how everything was arranged."

"You think someone's been in the house?" Jace asked quietly. Too quietly.

Liz gave a nervous little laugh. "Of course not. I just forgot to clean up after myself, that's all. Besides, how could someone get in and me not know about it?"

Jace nodded, but his contemplative withdrawal left Liz more uneasy than ever.

They ate, and after breakfast Jace insisted on helping her tidy up. When he suggested they pack a picnic and head up into the mountains for the remainder of the day, she agreed. Every moment spent with Jace was a moment in heaven.

It wasn't until Liz was ready to go that she realized Daisy was missing. She went outside and called the dog, but to no avail. Then it hit her that she hadn't seen Daisy since Jace's arrival the evening before.

Her pronouncement a few minutes later that her dog was missing met with a strange reaction from Jace.

"What dog, Lizzie? You don't have a dog."

"I do now," she muttered.

Jace folded his arms across his chest, speaking to her with all the patience of a parent talking to a fanciful child. "What kind of dog is it?"

"Golden retriever."

Jace blinked. "Wasn't that dog you accused me of having a golden retriever?"

"Well, I thought she *was* yours," Liz said defensively. "She was on your porch, then in your yard. What was I supposed to think?"

"You were supposed to believe me when I told you I didn't have a dog. Did you check her tags or the pound? Maybe she belongs to someone who's reported her lost."

"Daisy didn't have any tags and I didn't think to call the pound," she admitted.

"Daisy?"

"That's what I named her."

Jace glanced at the bouquet of white daisies on her kitchen table. "Favorite flower?"

Liz followed his gaze, wondering if she should tell him.

"Lizzie?"

Her eyes shot back to him. "Goldie always wanted a golden retriever," she said. "She wanted to name it Daisy."

"You really loved my grandmother, didn't you?"

Liz nodded miserably. She'd become way too attached to Daisy in just a few short days, too. If the dog had run away or gone back to her owner, Liz didn't know if she could handle it. Then another thought struck her. "You don't think Daisy's lying hurt somewhere, do you?"

Jace pulled her into the security of his arms. "Since Daisy just recently turned up in the neighborhood, I think she's a wanderer. She probably went out for a walk and found a boyfriend somewhere."

Liz considered that doubtfully.

"We had a female spaniel when I was growing up," he said. "As I recall, when she was in heat, she yowled a lot and wanted outside all the time. Is that the way Daisy is?"

Liz shook her head.

"Well, I'm sure she's okay. Let's get going and I'll bet by the time you get home, Daisy will be at your doorstep waiting for you."

Hours later, Jace was proved right. Almost.

Jace had returned to his place and Liz to hers. When she walked in the door Daisy *was* waiting for her—in front of the TV in the den watching "60 Minutes."

Six

Chester B. Griffith saw Liz the next morning without an appointment. In her limited experience, lawyers didn't see clients at the drop of a hat. She wondered if he actually worked or was just a figurehead.

Griffith smiled a welcome, but this time, it didn't quite reach his eyes. Knowing he was put out with her for not giving him an answer about the lawsuit against Jace and his family, she told him her decision immediately.

"It's your business, of course," he said, "but I think you're making a mistake."

"Maybe, but it's my mistake to make." She fiddled with her purse strap for a moment. "I need to ask you some questions about Goldie."

Chester glanced at his watch.

"I'll be brief," she promised. "You seem to be the only person around who knew Goldie for any length of time, Mr. Griffith, so I'm hoping you can shed some light on a matter I don't understand."

He quirked an eyebrow, but said nothing.

Liz forged ahead. "I'd like to know why Goldie cut herself off from her children."

"I don't really see that's any of your concern, Liz."

"I think she made it my concern when she left me her estate, Mr. Griffith," she said, annoyed at his attitude. "Now, do you or don't you know what caused the estrangement?"

The lawyer picked a piece of lint off his custom-made silk suit, then studied his hand-sewn leather shoes for a few moments. At last he met her gaze directly. "They were going to have her declared incompetent in order to take over her finances."

Liz stared at him, aghast. She didn't believe it for one moment and she said so.

Griffith rose and stalked across the room, then turned and gave Liz a pitying look. "Come now, Liz, these are the same people who are suing you for Goldie's estate. Doesn't that tell you anything?" He shook his head in disgust. "Goldie told me you were naive, but I had no idea just how naive."

That hurt. "I have one other question, Mr. Griffith."

"Yes?"

"How fast can I give away all the money Goldie left me?"

Chester B. Griffith frowned. "Give it away? What in the world are you talking about?"

Liz reached into her purse and pulled out a piece of paper. "This is how I want it divvied up."

Liz considered the other crucial item on her mental list of priorities. Despite her sabbatical from the university, she still had friends there. In particular, a friend at the art museum on campus who might be able to help her get a lead on the sugar cup.

Even though she had made her decision about how Goldie's estate should be distributed, she felt a little guilty about keeping what was probably a valuable artifact. Still, returning stolen property, even after all these years, could be awkward. She especially didn't want any undue publicity for Jace's family.

Henri Dubois was the artifacts curator at the museum. A natty man in his early fifties, he had immigrated to the United States with his family just after World War II. The museum was his life, ancient art his passion.

After exchanged pleasantries, Liz withdrew the vase from a box she pulled from her tote bag and carefully peeled away the layers of tissue paper. Then she lifted it out and held it in front of Henri's eyes.

At first the curator looked stunned. Then he gasped. Then he began to chatter in his native tongue. Liz couldn't understand a word.

"Henri, please!" she begged. "In English, and slow down."

The curator cradled the vase reverently. *"C'est magnifique!* Where have you discovered it?"

"You recognize it?" Liz asked.

"Mais, oui. If this is what I believe it to be, it is priceless!"

Liz was sitting on Jace's front porch when he came home.

He pulled his Jeep Cherokee into the garage, then came around front. He stood looking down at her, a smile of pleasure on his face. He reached out and stroked her cheek. "I've been thinking about you," he said softly.

Liz blinked up at him in surprise. "You have?"

He nodded. His eyes dropped to her mouth, where, unthinkingly, she was chewing on her lower lip.

"Did you miss me?"

"Jace, I..."

He took her hand and pulled her up. "Let's go inside, Lizzie, before I embarrass both of us."

Bemused, Liz went with him. She had spent the entire afternoon with Henri discussing the sugar cup. Her excitement level had reached new heights while she'd waited for Jace to come home, and now, when she had incredible news to tell him, he had only one thing on his mind. It was on her mind, too, but so was being relieved of this secret about a priceless object.

"We need to talk," she told him.

"We will," he growled, slamming the door shut behind them. "Later."

"Jace, if you think I came over here to climb into bed with you—" He silenced her with his mouth and Liz forgot her protest.

Somehow they made it up the stairs to his bedroom. Liz made a last-ditch effort at conversation, but before she could form the words, Jace had her clothes off and then his. From then on, she was too busy feeling to think.

Jace took her with a ferocity that excited her and defied anything she'd ever experienced before. She was shocked that, once she'd had a taste of him, it only got better.

"Oh, Lizzie, what you do to me," Jace panted as he lay on top of her, momentarily sated.

Liz ran her hands up and down his sweat-slicked back. Their bodies smelled of the scent of their lovemaking, and it was the most erotic intoxicating aroma she could imagine. It made her want him all over again, immediately. "You give back as good as you get, Jace," she murmured, and followed up her words by licking his shoulder.

Jace shuddered. His beard-roughened chin rasped against her skin as he nibbled his way down to her breast. He laved and nipped the tip, sending her into renewed spasms. "There's not a place on you that doesn't respond to me," he said in wonder.

Liz agreed as he continued his gentle exploration of her body.

"It's not fair I have to wait so long between times," he said, kissing his way down to her thighs. "I guess I'll have to make love to you some other way." And he did.

It was dark when Liz awoke. In some ways, she hated the time afterward, the time of thinking. She was her own worst enemy when she had too much time to think.

This was one of those times.

Liz was almost afraid of the feelings she had for Jace. Nothing in her life had ever lasted, and she had no reason to believe a relationship with Jace would, either. If she began to care too deeply, she would be letting herself in for a world of hurt.

She glanced at the clock on his nightstand, reluctant to wake him, but knowing they had to talk about the sugar cup. "Jace?" She rubbed her hand across his chest. He murmured in his sleep, but didn't awaken. "Jace, wake up." Her hand roamed lower. She discovered that part of him was awake, anyway.

"Lizzie, I don't know if I can keep up with you, honey."

She grinned. "You're definitely keeping up, buster, but that's not why I want you awake. I want to talk to you."

Jace fumbled with the light, switching it on. Both of them were temporarily blinded.

"We could've talked in the dark," Liz groused. She opened her eyes to find Jace staring at her breasts.

"No, we couldn't have."

Liz reached for the sheet, but Jace stilled her hand.

"I can't get you out of my mind, Lizzie. The least you can do is let me look."

Liz felt her face grow warm, more with desire than embarrassment. "I'm a little chilly," she lied.

"No problem." He pulled her up against him, but made certain the sheet was still around her waist. "Talk."

Liz caught herself absently twirling the springy hair on his chest. She started to pull her hand away, but Jace captured it in his own. "Don't stop."

This intimacy was new to Liz. Jace was evidently a man who was proud of his body, of how his body felt when she touched him, and he wanted to make sure she knew it. Just as he wanted her to know how much pleasure he derived from something as simple as just looking at her. She offered him a brilliant smile. "I won't."

"So, what's got you all worked up?"

"I wouldn't say I'm worked up, exactly," Liz said, but she couldn't keep the excitement from her voice.

"I could see to it that you are," he promised softly.

"Jace . . ." The temptation to forget about the sugar cup, forget about what she'd decided to do with the money, was strong. Jace's fingers worked a magic on her that made her want to forget everything but him.

He smiled indulgently, rubbing his hand up and down her arm. "Okay, talk."

"I went to see a friend of mine at the university art museum," she said. "His name is Henri Dubois. He's the artifacts curator." She squirmed, raising up on her elbow, causing Jace to wince when she jabbed his chest. "Sorry." She kissed the spot she'd injured. "Henri recognized the sugar cup, Jace. He thinks it's from the Ming Dynasty— over six hundred years old!"

"What's a sugar cup?"

Liz looked at him with a silly grin on her face. "Remember I told you Goldie loaned me sugar?"

He nodded.

"Well, she used to put it in this little vase because it held exactly two cups."

Jace stilled her hand against his chest. "My grandmother let you borrow sugar in a Ming vase?"

"Incredible, isn't it?"

"Stupid is more like it. What does that mean it's worth?"

Forgetting her nakedness, Liz scooted up against the headboard, crossing her legs beneath the sheet. "Henri wasn't sure, but he guessed a million."

Jace stared at her as if he'd never seen her before. "A million dollars?"

Liz nodded. "I couldn't believe it, either. I mean, I told Goldie's attorney I wanted to get rid of all the money and other assets she left to me, but since I've decided to keep the sugar cup, I didn't include it in the list I gave him. Which isn't going to make him too happy when he finds out, since he asked me about it specifically. I never dreamed it would be worth so much."

Jace's face went to stone. He, too, sat up. "What do you mean 'get rid of all the money'? What have you done, Liz?"

Liz felt a tremor of uneasiness shimmer up her back. "I didn't want what she left me, Jace. I told Mr. Griffith to give it away."

She could almost see Jace mentally counting to ten. His beautiful blue eyes went to ice, and his fists bunched until his knuckles turned white. "What did you tell him to do with the money, Liz?"

Suddenly uncomfortable in Jace's bed, Liz slid out from beneath the covers and groped for her clothes. "I asked him to set up an auction to sell all the antiques. The proceeds from that, and whatever is left after trusts are set up for—"

"Hell." Jace ran his long fingers through his hair. "I can't believe this."

Liz finished buttoning her blouse. She lifted her chin in defiance. "She left me the money, Jace. I can do whatever I want with it." She wiped at the single tear running down her cheek. "I mistakenly thought you would approve."

With that, Liz grabbed her purse and shoes and ran from the room and out of the house.

The pounding on her front door began less than two minutes later.

"Lizzie, open the damned door!"

Liz looked at Daisy, who stared back at her with alert interest.

"I may ruin my damned shoulder trying, but I'll break it down if you don't unlock it," Jace warned.

Liz didn't doubt him for a moment. The thought of his beautiful body injured in any way was enough to send her flying to the door. She threw it open, but didn't step out of the way fast enough to avoid Jace's body as it hurtled through the opening.

Liz went down hard on the wood floor. Her head hit it with a sickening crack. She blinked up at Jace, but there were too many of him to focus on. She heard him calling her name. For some strange reason, her mouth wouldn't cooperate to answer.

She thought she felt Daisy lick her cheek, but when she opened her eyes again, there were still only Jaces leaning over her. It surprised her to think she saw concern on all his faces. He couldn't be concerned—he was angry with her. She had given away Goldie's money, and from his reaction a short time ago, the money was all he really cared about.

Liz closed her eyes, willing away the pain, willing away yet another deception.

She moaned and tried to pull away from the offensive light shining in her eyes, but at the slightest movement, steel girders dropped on her head. "Dammit, leave me alone," she mumbled.

"I'd say she's okay," said a voice she didn't recognize.

"Well, her mouth works, anyway," contributed another, laced with humor.

"Should she go to the hospital?"

Finally a voice Liz recognized. Jace's. She forced her eyes open. Like an avenging angel, he was hovering over the two paramedics bent over her.

"She may have a concussion. We can either transport her, or you can find someone to stay here with her and check on her periodically during the night."

"What do you want to do, Lizzie?" Jace asked.

"I can tend to myself."

"Like hell," Jace snarled softly. "She stays and I watch her," he informed the paramedics. "Tell me what to do."

After the two men left, Jace carried Liz up the stairs. She couldn't help thinking how different the circumstances were this time.

Jace began to undress her, but she batted his hands away. "I can do it."

"I'm sure you can, but *I'm* going to."

"Jace…"

"Lizzie," he mocked. He had her stripped in no time flat, then gently eased a nightgown over her head. "They left something for the headache. Climb into bed and I'll get some water."

Which reminded Liz. "Will you give Daisy some fresh water and feed her?"

He opened his mouth, evidently thought better of what he'd been about to say and grunted something that could have been either acquiescence or skepticism.

"Here," Jace said several minutes later. "I'll help you sit up while you drink."

Liz was thirsty, but the moment the water hit her stomach, she had the urge to run to the bathroom.

"Take it easy," Jace said. "Just a little." He pulled the glass away and lowered her against the pillow. "Try and sleep now."

Liz closed her eyes. "Won't I die or something if I go to sleep?"

"No, Lizzie, you're going to be fine."

"Did you feed Daisy?"

Jace didn't respond, and Liz forced her eyes open. "I forgot to tell you where her dishes are."

"I found them," he said. "They were both full."

Liz frowned. "Daisy always cleans her bowl up by this time."

"Go to sleep, honey. Your mysterious dog will be fine."

Liz dozed off wondering why Jace thought Daisy was mysterious. Just because she seemed to walk through walls and operate the remote control for the TV didn't make her mysterious. . . .

Seven

Jace served Liz breakfast in bed the next morning. Nothing elaborate—just toast, oatmeal and a glass of orange juice—but it was the best breakfast Liz had ever tasted.

As she nibbled on her toast, she watched Jace where he sat sprawled in the chair nearest the window. His cheeks and chin were dark with stubble, his hair tousled and spiky, as if he'd run his fingers through it a hundred times. His eyes were an especially vibrant blue against the bleary red road maps surrounding them. On him it looked good. On her, well, she was surprised he hadn't run screaming from the room.

"Want anything else?" he asked. He closed his eyes and laced his fingers together over his stomach.

"No, thank you," she said, her tone polite if a little stiff. "This was wonderful."

He opened his eyes to slits. "It's pretty simple fare."

Liz looked down at her plate, miserable in the ensuing silence.

"Why give all that money away when you could've kept it?" he finally asked.

"Jace, please. She left it to me. I can do whatever I want with it."

His gaze was still hooded, but the tenseness of his body told her just how alert he was. "I know that, Lizzie. I just want you to think it through before you finalize anything."

Liz had to try to make him understand. "Your grandmother was involved in drugs, prostitution and gambling—all things that ruin people's lives. How could I keep money she earned that way?"

Jace stared at her as if he'd never seen her before. "My grandmother wasn't a criminal!"

Liz frowned. "Mr. Griffith told me she took over Giovanni's business when he died. He said—"

"Giovanni's business? You think he was some kind of mafia kingpin, Lizzie?"

That was exactly what she thought.

"Hell, my grandfather was an errand boy, honey. He screwed up and they offed him. Plain and simple."

Liz's mouth fell open in shock.

Jace stood, shaking his head in disbelief. He rammed his hands into the back pockets of his jeans and turned to stare out the window.

Liz set aside the tray and threw back the covers. She sat up, fighting a wave of dizziness. Gingerly she rose from the bed and padded across the carpet to where he stood. "Jace, if Goldie wasn't doing anything illegal, how did she get all that money?"

"My grandmother inherited money that filtered down from moonshine operations during Prohibition."

"Moonshine?"

Jace nodded.

"That means Chester Griffith *lied* to me."

"He probably believes all the rumors he's heard about her."

"I don't understand any of this."

"I haven't helped matters any, have I?" He reached out to stroke her cheek.

Liz leaned into his hand, nuzzling it, taking comfort in his touch.

"My grandmother evidently had a head for investments, and what started out as half a million dollars ended up multiplied several times."

"So you got *your* head for investments through the genetic grapevine."

Jace looked startled for a moment, then he flashed a lopsided smile. "I guess I did."

Liz put her arms around him. "You and Goldie would have hit it off so well." She chose her next words carefully. "Mr. Griffith told me why your grandmother split from your family."

Jace pulled back to peer down at her.

"He said your mother and uncles were trying to have her committed and then sue for trusteeship of her estate."

Jace stood in momentary stunned silence. When at last he spoke, he roared. "*What?* That's the most asinine thing I've ever heard!"

He gave Liz a shake, forgetting that her head still wasn't quite functioning properly. She grimaced with pain, but he didn't seem to notice.

"What if it's true?" he finally asked, his tone dull.

Liz put her hands on his wrists and he loosened his grasp. "I don't think it is."

"How do you know?" he countered bitterly. "My family's got a lawsuit going against you. If anyone needed proof that they're a bunch of vultures, this is it."

Liz met his gaze unflinchingly. "I've learned that I'm not the world's greatest judge of character, but I've met your mom and your uncles, Jace. I just can't believe they would do something like that to their own mother."

"They were close to reconciling with my grandmother before she died," he admitted. "They'd been talking, ironing things out, they said. That's how Mom came to find her that morning."

"That must have been the surprise Goldie told me about."

Jace raked his fingers through his hair. "I'm damned well going to find out if what he said is true." Without another word, he left the room.

The echo of his thundering footsteps and the slamming door stayed with Liz for a long time.

Liz sat three stairs up from the bottom, her elbow propped on her knee, her chin cradled in the palm of her hand, staring at the sugar cup. Henri had verified its authenticity. Now she was waiting to hear about its history.

Thanks to Jace, her faith in Goldie had been restored, but because of Chester B. Griffith, she had an entirely new set of questions that needed answers.

She didn't believe for a minute that Goldie's children had conspired to have her put away so they could get at her money. And suing her estate now that Goldie was dead wasn't the same thing, no matter what Griffith or Jace thought.

Daisy whimpered. Liz absently patted her head, directing her full attention to the dog when Daisy put her head on her knee.

"You're as big a puzzle as the sugar cup, Daisy. Every time I look for you when Jace is here, you've disappeared."

Daisy tilted her head in an inquisitive manner.

"Is Jace right? Do you have a doggie friend?"

Daisy's tail thumped against the leg of the Shaker table. The table wobbled, rocking the Ming vase.

"Careful, girl. Your tail could be a dangerous weapon." Liz scooted down a step so Daisy's head rested in her lap. "What do you think, Daisy? Is Jace's whole family nuts? Is Chester B. Griffith a liar?" She looked directly into Daisy's intelligent eyes. "Are you for real?"

Daisy woofed, but which of Liz's questions she was answering, and whether her answer was yes or no, would remain a mystery. With a sigh, Liz went back to studying the sugar cup. "My friend at the museum is supposed to call today and let me know what he found out about the theft. I ought to return it to its rightful owner, but to tell you the truth, I don't want to."

For the remainder of the day, Liz made a desultory effort to relax, but she was so wired she couldn't sit still. Her headache had been tempered to a dull throb, but any sudden motion sent her into a tailspin.

She tried reading a book, and after focusing on the same page for ten minutes, she gave up. She turned on the TV, but the afternoon talk shows made her crazy.

Talking to Griffith later, trying to pin him down on the status of the instructions she had left with him, was an effort in futility. He made all the right responses, but something was amiss. Liz couldn't quite put her finger on what, but she was beginning to have a very bad feeling about him.

Finally, in a fit of pique because she'd heard from neither Jace nor Henri, she went to the kitchen and gathered the ingredients for baking cookies.

Forty-five minutes later she sat down and ate a dozen, warm from the oven, with a glass of milk. When the phone rang, she was seriously thinking about working on the next dozen.

"Liz, it's Henri."

"It's about time!"

Henri chuckled. "Always in a hurry, *ma petite*. The Ming is over six hundred years old. A few days is not so much time to learn its history."

"Sorry," Liz said. "I'm not my usual cheery self today."

"Are you ill?"

"I fell and hit my head," she explained. "I'm okay, but I have a headache."

"Shall I phone back later?"

"No! Henri, tell me—I can't stand the suspense."

Henri's reverent sigh carried over the line. "It belonged to an emperor, Liz. It was stolen from him and turned up later, once in a Russian czar's palace, and once in the castle of a king of England."

"And?"

"After about 1480, it was never seen again."

"Fourteen-eighty?" Liz squawked.

"*Oui.* It is the only one of its kind, Liz, which is perhaps why it disappeared after only a hundred years."

"Good Lord."

"No one's had any knowledge of where it's been all this time."

"Until it got to the museum."

"*Non.*"

It took a moment for Liz to digest that. "The Ming was never in a museum?"

"Because of what you told me, I contacted every museum in France known to house antiquities. None had ever heard of that particular Ming being in a museum—anywhere." He paused. "Naturally, word will spread that I was asking, but I seriously doubt any new information will come forth."

"He lied to me about that, too," Liz muttered under her breath.

"Pardon?"

"Nothing. Just talking to myself."

"Um, Liz, you will tell me how you obtained the Ming?"

"I will, Henri," she promised, "but I'm afraid I can't right now."

He sighed. "Very well, but I must say, this find, it is *extraordinaire.* You own a priceless work of art."

"As priceless as you originally thought?"

"*Non,* more. Several million dollars, at least."

Swell, Liz thought as she hung up. No wonder Chester B. Griffith was so hot to find out where it was.

Jace checked in on Liz around eight. He hadn't shaved, and his expression was haggard, but he was the most precious sight she'd ever seen.

He took her lips in a breath-stealing kiss, then drew her into a crushing embrace.

"Rough day?" she guessed.

"I swear, if I could put myself out for adoption right now, I would."

"It can't be that bad."

"Worse."

Liz pulled away from him and closed the door. "Maybe you'd better tell me."

"You're not going to like it."

She grimaced wryly. "It won't be the first thing I haven't liked recently." She looked around. "Did Daisy go out when I let you in?"

Jace rammed his fingers through his hair. "I didn't see any damned dog, Liz!"

"You don't have to get testy." Liz whirled, leaving him in her wake as she stormed to the kitchen.

"What are you doing?" he asked, helping himself to a cold soda.

Stiff with annoyance, Liz kept her back to him. "Making you something to eat."

Jace paused in the midst of opening his can. "How did you know I was hungry?"

Liz looked at him over her shoulder, one eyebrow arched in mockery. "Don't all men get cranky on an empty stomach?"

Jace grinned sheepishly. "Sorry. I shouldn't take my anger at my family out on you."

"True." She pointed toward the table. "Sit and tell me about it while I make you a sandwich."

With a sigh, Jace did as he was told. He took a long swallow of his soda before he spoke. "They were all furious when I told them Griffith's story about their wanting to have Goldie committed."

"Why does that surprise you? Anyone would be furious that he lied."

"I thought so at first, too, but while Mom, Tony, Joe and I were discussing this, Dad came in and reminded them that, in a fit of anger, they had considered doing exactly that when she told all of them it was time to earn their own livings."

Liz turned to face him. "Oh, no!"

Jace nodded, his expression grim. "Not only did they consider it, they talked to an attorney about it."

"I doubt it was Griffith," Liz said, "but I'll bet you're going to tell me it was an Osborne." An image of the sign outside the law office flashed through Liz's mind.

Jace stared at her in astonishment. "How did you know?"

She shrugged. "It was the only way Griffith could have known. Any other attorney would have respected client confidentiality. If his partners are anything like him, they're pond scum."

Jace gave a bark of laughter. "Lizzie, you amaze me."

She smiled beatifically and turned back to making his sandwich. "I want to meet with your family, Jace. I want to talk to them, explain to them about the money, why I gave it away." She picked up the knife and sliced neatly through the concoction in front of her. "I owe them that much."

"I don't think that's such a good idea, honey. Especially since my grandmother didn't do the things that made you decide to give it away."

Liz slid the knife under the sandwich and lifted it onto a plate. She scooped potato salad from the bowl, added some pickle slices and Fritos and set the plate in front of him. "I don't think it's for you to say, Jace," she said softly.

"Dammit, Liz, you don't know who you're dealing with."

"That's right, I don't. But I want to, and I want to do it on my own."

Jace scowled at her.

"Playing Mr. Tough Guy won't sway me, Jace. I've made up my mind."

"You're still planning on giving away the money even though you know Goldie was on the up-and-up?"

No matter how she said it, her decision was going to inflame him. "What I do with that money is up to me."

Jace put his sandwich back on the plate. "So, butt out, huh?"

Liz sighed and covered his fist with her hand. "It's a moot point. According to Mr. Griffith, it's a done deal."

"No offense, Lizzie, but letting the shyster lawyer of the century handle my grandmother's fortune could be a mistake. I have cousins who could have used that money."

"He has nothing to say about it, Jace. Every one of the organizations I selected is worthwhile, and—"

"Did that salve your conscience?"

Liz recoiled as if he had struck her. "I didn't do it to make *myself* feel better."

Regret and shame chased each other across Jace's features. "Liz, I—"

"Don't you dare apologize, Jace. I wouldn't want you to add hypocritical to your list of otherwise sterling qualities."

"Dammit, Liz, I'm trying to tell you I'm sorry. You have every right to do whatever you want with the money."

"Gee, thanks."

He went on, ignoring her sarcasm. "I'm just asking you to think things over now that you know Goldie wasn't a criminal."

Liz busied herself cleaning up the counter. "Eat your dinner, then I think you'd better go." When she was done, she went to the door, opened it and whistled for Daisy. After several minutes of no response, she gave up. She turned to find Jace staring at her.

"Do you do that often?" he asked.

"Do what?"

"Whistle for a dog I've never seen?"

"Just because Daisy is off roaming the neighborhood every time you come over doesn't mean she doesn't exist."

"Did I say she doesn't exist?"

"You implied it."

Jace sighed. "I don't want to argue with you, Lizzie."

"Then why are you?" Liz was angry, but worse was the painful ache caused by his doubt.

"I don't want to see you get hurt."

"And you think I will be if I meet with your family?"

"They won't mean to, but blood's thicker than water, Lizzie. They're looking out for their kids' futures."

Finally she knew how he felt about family ties. "So am I."

Eight

Jace wanted to spend the night. Liz wanted him to stay, too, but she wasn't going to cave in to her hormones.

If Jace stayed, she wouldn't be thinking about anything but him, and there were too many other things running around in her mind that needed her concentration.

She sent him on his way, feeling as if she'd just kicked a puppy. "Speaking of puppies," she muttered, opening the door a short time later, "where's that darned dog?"

In answer to her question, Daisy woofed from the head of the stairs. Liz stepped back inside and whirled around. "Daisy, why didn't you come when I called you earlier? Don't you like Jace?"

Daisy dashed down the stairs, tail flying. She came perilously close to the Shaker table. "Settle down, girl," Liz said, kneeling beside the excited dog. "I'm glad to see you, too. Where have you been?" Daisy danced against the hardwood floor in the foyer, her claws clicking excitedly. "Upstairs, huh? Hungry?"

Daisy barked in response.

"C'mon, then."

Liz put food and water into Daisy's bowls, then went up to change into her nightgown. Though it was still early, she opted to read in bed.

Several hours later, she came awake with a jerk. Disoriented, she couldn't remember for a moment why the light beside the bed was still on. Then she realized she had dozed off reading, which didn't explain what had awakened her or why Daisy was whining downstairs.

The dog's whine escalated into a growl. The hair on the back of Liz's neck stood at attention. She'd never thought of Daisy as a watchdog, but there was something about the snarling sound that told Liz in no uncertain terms that something was wrong.

Suddenly she heard the sound of breaking glass. She instinctively reached over to turn off the light. Before her feet hit the floor, Daisy was at her side.

"Good girl, Daisy." Liz groped for the phone on her bedside table, grateful it had a lighted key pad. It never occurred to her to dial 911. It also never occurred to her to wonder how she remembered Jace's phone number when she hadn't dialed it more than once or twice. He answered on the first ring.

"What?" he barked in greeting.

If Liz hadn't thought her life was in jeopardy, she'd have hung up on him. As it was, she ignored his sour disposition and whispered into the receiver, "Jace, someone's trying to get in. I heard glass breaking."

She started to say more, but Jace cut her off. "Where are you, Lizzie?"

"In my bedroom."

"Stay put, honey. I'll be right there." She never even heard him hang up.

Liz crawled behind the easy chair in the corner. Daisy followed.

Jace made his appearance moments later. Through her open window, Liz heard him barreling across the lawn and up the porch. He swore as he tried the doorknob and found it locked. She lost track of him as he took off around the house.

Several minutes later, following a loud commotion, footsteps pounded up the stairs. Liz pressed farther into the corner, clasping Daisy around the neck. Where was Jace?

Liz was sorry she'd ever exchanged a cross word with him. He couldn't help the family he'd been born into. He was a loyal son, trying to ease the rift between her, as Goldie's friend, and his mother and uncles. She admired his loyalty and dedication. She loved him and she wanted him safe.

Liz clutched Daisy even more tightly as the footsteps seemed to increase in volume and velocity. What she should have done was call the police.

"Lizzie, where are you, babe?"

Liz could have broken down and cried. She might have if she hadn't been so scared. "Jace?"

The light went on. "Liz?"

Liz released Daisy and crawled out from behind the chair. "Here." She stood, not quite believing her eyes when saw the man whose collar Jace was gripping in his mighty fist. "It's your uncle!" she gasped.

"I thought you'd remember Tony," Jace said dryly. "He dropped by to pay you a visit, only he forgot to knock. Didn't you, Tony?" Jace gave his uncle a shake, and though the older man's stature equaled his, Tony's body undulated with the force.

"You were trying to break into my house?" Liz was furious now that her fear was beginning to abate.

Jace shot her a grim look. "He wasn't just trying, honey. He did."

"What do you want?" she cried.

"The Ming vase," Tony said, his expression sullen and maybe even a little embarrassed.

"Damn you!" Jace bellowed.

Tony shook himself free of his nephew's grasp. "It's worth a lot of money and *she*—" he pointed an accusing finger at Liz "—has it."

"So what if she does? Goldie left her everything. If she has it, she came by it legally." Jace never took his eyes off his uncle. "You want to call the cops, Lizzie? Press charges?"

Liz considered it. Seriously. Tony Fabrizio had scared her witless. He deserved to get a little of his own back, and a night in jail might be just the thing. She opened her mouth to say yes, but couldn't quite bring herself to do something like that to one of Jace's relatives.

He must have read her decision. "Don't be lenient on my account, Lizzie. Tony's acting like a criminal, so he ought to be treated like one."

"I—" Liz began.

"Throw me in the slammer if you want to!" Tony shouted. "Once this lawsuit is settled, you won't have anything, anyway."

Liz almost hated to burst his bubble. For some reason, she liked Tony. Probably because he reminded her of Jace. "Tony, I don't want you arrested, but I do want you and Joe and Anna and me to talk about this like reasonable adults."

Tony eyed her suspiciously, then glanced at Jace.

Jace's features tightened. "Don't look at me. I'm against it. I don't think she owes any of you anything."

"Is that any way to talk to family?" Tony growled.

"I'm not too proud that you *are* family right now," Jace told him.

Tony squirmed, unable to meet his nephew's intent gaze. "I think I can find my own way out."

"I'll show you, just in case," Jace said. "And Liz will be sending you the bill for the window repair."

Tony scowled, but didn't protest.

The moment the two of them disappeared down the stairs, Liz felt Daisy's tongue against her hand. "Lovely life we lead, huh?"

Daisy butted her body against Liz's legs in response.

"C'mon, girl, let's go see what the damage is."

Liz was inspecting the mangled multipaned window when Jace appeared on the other side. She gave a startled gasp before she realized it was him.

"I'm going to put a piece of plywood over it," Jace explained. "You can't sleep in the house with the window wide open."

Liz didn't argue with him. In fact, she didn't want to sleep in the house at all. Even though her burglar had been Jace's uncle, she still didn't feel particularly safe. "Would you, uh, like to come in for a cup of hot chocolate when you're through?"

Hammer in hand, Jace said around the nails in his mouth, "Sure."

With an inward sigh, Liz headed for the kitchen. Maybe if Jace hung around awhile, her nerves would settle down and she could get to sleep.

A short time later, Liz amended that thought. Maybe if Jace hung around awhile, he'd hang around all night. She didn't want to be alone. Seeing him standing there, looking more sexy and appealing than he had a right to look in faded jeans that clung to every beautiful inch below the waist and a T-shirt that just as nicely took care of every inch above, left her with only one thought on her mind.

She offered him a tentative smile.

"I need to wash up," he said.

Liz nodded.

Jace didn't move.

She wondered what he read in her eyes. A moment later, pressed against his body, she knew.

"I don't really want hot chocolate," he muttered against her lips.

"Neither do I."

"Good."

Jace was gone when Liz awoke. A note was taped to the bathroom mirror. "Called glass shop for window repair. Taking you out to dinner. Be ready at 7. J." Liz grinned. Such a *personal* note.

The repairman showed up soon after Liz finished breakfast. With Daisy beside her, she read the paper while he worked in the other room. An hour later, he popped his head into the kitchen to say he was done, packed up his tools and was gone within minutes.

With the rest of the day ahead of her, Liz decided to return the books she'd borrowed from the library. After that, she visited Henri at the museum, but he had no new information for her.

Her phone was ringing when she got home. She fumbled with the lock, ended up dropping half of what she was carrying, but managed to grab the receiver on the fourth ring. "Hello," she said breathlessly.

"Liz?"

"Yes."

"This is Anna McGuinn." Jace's mother sounded even younger on the phone than she looked. "Tony told me about last night. I'm not excusing him, but I thought you might want to know what's behind his behavior."

Liz didn't know whether to punt or bite. She bit. "Actually, I would."

Anna's sigh of relief carried over the line. "Are you free now? Would you like to come over for coffee?"

Liz glanced at her watch. Jace wasn't due to pick her up for another three hours. That left plenty of time to visit with Anna, get home for a quick shower and change. "Sure. What's your address?"

"I'm so glad you came," Anna said warmly. "I was afraid Tony had turned you against all of us permanently with that stunt he pulled last night."

Liz lifted the delicate fluted cup to her lips and sipped. She looked Anna in the eye and said bluntly, "I haven't gotten the impression that you and Joe are as gung ho for this lawsuit as Tony."

Anna examined her nails briefly. "I was at first—not because of the money, you understand. As you can see—" she waved her fingers gracefully through the air "—my husband and I live comfortably. We don't need my mother's money."

"Then why?"

Anna chewed her Sophia Loren lower lip in distress. When she met Liz's gaze again, her huge brown eyes were filled with tears. "For Tony, or more specifically, Tony's wife."

"I don't understand."

Anna gave her a watery smile. "No, of course you don't. Tony's wife has leukemia and needs a bone-marrow transplant. The medical costs are exorbitant, and they have no insurance."

"I didn't know," Liz murmured.

"None of us knew. He and Sheila kept it from everyone except their children."

"They should have told you," Liz said, knowing how close this family was.

Anna put out a trembling hand and grasped Liz's fingers. "Yes, they should have, but they've been waiting to find out if one of their kids is a compatible donor."

"And is one?"

"No, the doctors look for a six-point match, but the best any of the children have is four."

"I'll test," Liz offered automatically.

"We'll all test now that we know, but that still doesn't help pay the bills. And if that isn't bad enough, there was a fire several months ago that destroyed their house and everything inside it. Tony and Sheila have been living in an apartment, fighting with the insurance company about paying off the loss."

Liz felt contemptible. "Why didn't Jace tell me?"

"He doesn't know about anything except the fire yet." Anna withdrew her hand and took a sip from her cup. "Jace is brilliant when it comes to finances, Liz. He put Tony on the right track of so many good investments that my brother should have been able to retire rich right now." She smiled sadly. "Tony has always been the kind of man who lives for adventure. Every penny he made in good solid investments went into some harebrained scheme that immediately lost money."

"I don't know what I can do, Anna."

"You can give him the money he needs to get Sheila the transplant and get back on his feet. None of us has enough in cash savings to help him."

"I would if I could," Liz said miserably. Why hadn't she thought to ask Jace's uncles or his mother if they needed anything? She had only considered their children and grandchildren.

Anna's dark eyes grew frosty. "After all the wonderful things Jace has told me about you, I never figured you for a selfish woman."

Liz opened her mouth to defend herself, but Anna waved a hand to stave her off. "Forget I asked," she said.

"Anna, I'd help him if I could."

"*If?*" She raked Liz with a derisive glance that made Liz feel like dirt. "I just hope my son wakes up before you suck him up with that blushing-virgin act of yours." By then, Anna was at the door, holding it open.

Liz left, certain her heart had just been ripped out.

It didn't surprise her when Jace called ten minutes before he was due to pick her up to say he couldn't make it.

What did surprise her was how much it hurt that he had so little faith in her.

Liz tried reading the novel she'd picked up at the library, but gave up after the first chapter when she realized she hadn't a clue about what she'd read.

There was no solace in television, either, but there was in Daisy. Liz talked and Daisy listened, offering an occasional woof or whine of commiseration. Between the two of them, Liz figured out how to help Tony's wife.

Life had been so simple three months ago.

Liz felt the first hot tear course down her cheek, but she didn't have much time to cry and feel sorry for herself—the lights went off without so much as a warning flicker.

Daisy, still sitting by her knee, tensed and growled. The sound was so frightening to Liz, who knew and loved the dog, that she almost felt sorry for whomever Daisy sensed.

Before Liz could decide what to do, the dog was off like a shot. The next sound Liz heard was the patio door sliding open. As she cursed herself for not having locked it, she realized that the intruder must have sabotaged her electrical box. He meant to harm her.

Liz knew she had the advantage. She was familiar with the layout of her house; the person who'd broken in wasn't. She reached the kitchen and lifted the receiver off the hook. The line was dead. She squelched the urge to moan in defeat at the same instant Daisy began to bark ferociously.

Liz grabbed the moment. She reached for the knob of the kitchen door, yanked it open and fled the house, which was what she knew she should have done in the first place.

Jace's house was dark, but unless he had changed the locks, she could find safety. Liz knew exactly where Goldie's spare key was hidden.

The raucous barking continued from her own house, spurring Liz on. She somehow managed to get the key into the lock, thanked God when it worked, and stumbled by waning moonlight to the phone on the counter in Jace's kitchen.

Dialing 911 was the most frustrating thing she'd ever done. Her fingers trembled so badly she could barely punch in the numbers. By the time the faceless voice came on the line, getting a coherent thought out of her mouth was a major effort.

She was absolutely certain she broke the dispatcher's eardrum with her scream when the lights came on in Jace's kitchen.

Nine

Liz had a new appreciation for a phrase she'd first heard in some horror movie as a child: dying of fright.

"What the hell!"

It took her a moment to realize the voice belonged to Jace. She crumpled to the floor, crying and babbling incoherently.

"Liz, for God's sake, what's the matter?" Jace knelt beside her, putting a protective arm around her. "Lizzie?"

"Someone's in my house," she managed between sobs. "The power went out, the phone wasn't working."

Jace swore violently. "Stay put, honey."

Liz grabbed the front of his shirt with a strength she didn't know she possessed. "Don't go," she begged. "I called the police. They're on their way." Even as she said the words, they both heard a loud popping noise repeated several times, followed by the squeal of tires on the street out front.

"The cops are here," Jace said grimly. "I'd better go tell them the burglar has a gun."

Until that moment, Liz hadn't realized what those popping sounds were. "No! If he has a gun, he might shoot you."

"I'll be fine."

She made a supreme effort to pull herself together. "Jace, please!"

"Lizzie, I'll be fine. Honest."

Liz couldn't rid herself of the notion that the intruder was bent on hurting someone. Shots had been fired, but no one had been in the house except Daisy. "Is it your uncle again? Do you think he's injured Daisy?"

"I just left Tony and Joe at Mom's."

"Thank God."

"I can't believe you've taken all this crap from my family and you're still sticking up for them."

"They're Goldie's flesh and blood!"

Jace pressed a quick hard kiss against her lips. "I have to go."

He was back almost before she knew he was gone. "Whoever it was got away." He hunkered down to where she still sat huddled in a corner of the kitchen floor. "They found blood on the floor in the den. Are you sure Daisy was in the house, Liz?"

Liz was dismayed that there had been an injury, but now that she'd had time to think about it, she wasn't particularly worried about the dog. Daisy seemed to be able to take care of herself. Liz was convinced the blood most likely belonged to the intruder. "She was, but she may have followed me out."

"This is one time I'm glad she pulled a disappearing act."

"I want to go home now."

He helped her up. "Just to answer a few questions for the police and to make sure things are locked up tight for the night, but then you're coming back here," he said firmly.

Liz looked up at him with a question in her eyes.

"I mean it, Lizzie."

"I know you do," she said. "What I can't figure out is why."

It took an hour for the two officers to ask their questions and locate the four bullets. It took another hour for Jace to check all the doors and windows and for Liz to ascertain that Daisy wasn't hiding in the house somewhere, as she had before.

By the time they got back to Jace's, it was close to midnight.

"You're sleeping with me," Jace said.

Weary and tired of never knowing exactly where she stood with him, Liz's eyes blazed. "Aren't you the same guy who called and canceled our date tonight after talking to Mommy?" She knew she sounded like a shrew, but at the moment she didn't particularly care.

Jace didn't bother to deny it. "My mother called, crying, saying she had an emergency. I didn't have a choice."

Liz had thought better of Jace's mother, but she couldn't fault Jace for responding to a family crisis. "And you're still talking to me after what she told you?"

Jace's beautiful blue eyes clouded with pain. "I'm still talking to you, but I'm not talking to her."

"Oh, no! Jace, you can't—she's your mother."

"Does that give her the right to distort everything to suit her own needs?"

"If Tony was there, you know that's not true."

Jace dragged his long fingers through his hair. "Dammit, Liz . . ."

"Let's go to bed," she urged softly. "We'll sort this out in the morning. I'm calling a confab with all the concerned parties, and there's nothing you can say to dissuade me."

For the next hour, and intermittently during the night, though Jace didn't try to change Liz's mind, he did his best to make her forget everything but him.

Liz wanted everyone to be as comfortable as possible. Her living room was large, and there was plenty of seating.

All her guests were right on time. She had dug out the silver service that had belonged to her mother, ostentatious as it was, and served everyone freshly ground coffee and cookies. Chocolate-chip cookies. Only Jace seemed to appreciate the irony of that.

Joe, who rarely said anything in her presence, spoke up first. "Elizabeth, er, Liz, I want you to know, I'm having my name removed from the lawsuit."

"You what?" Tony bellowed.

"I want my name off, too," Anna said.

Tony glared at her.

"Very sensible," Chester B. Griffith said, nodding his head. "I knew there was something of your mother in *some* of you."

"Shut up," Tony snarled.

Liz stood and passed around the cookie plate again. "Before you decide just what you're going to be doing in relation to the money Goldie left me, I think we should get a few things straight."

She went to stand in front of Anna. "First of all, I appreciate the loyalty you have for your brother. I envy you that you even *have* a brother to worry about. I just want you to know I don't hold any grudges as a result of our, um, conversation yesterday."

Anna's olive complexion took on a reddish tint.

Liz moved on to Joe. She smiled down at him. "I don't really know you, Joe, but I like you. I hope we're going to be friends."

Joe nodded, cast a worried sidelong glance at his older brother, then looked back at Liz and smiled. "Mama had a good friend in you, Liz. I'm glad."

"I think I was the lucky one, Joe, but thank you for saying so."

She stepped over to where Tony sat, kneeling down in front of him. "I'm more sorry than I can ever say about Sheila, Tony. If I'd known from the start about her illness, I never would have instructed Mr. Griffith to disburse the money Goldie left me like I did."

"Then get it back," Tony pleaded, swallowing what little was left of his pride.

Liz patted his knee. She rose and moved on to Jace. Despite the interested audience looking on, she reached out and stroked his cheek. Her heart was in her eyes for all to see. "If nothing else good comes of all this, the one thing I'll have had is the pleasure of knowing you," she said softly.

"Ditto," Jace whispered back, his voice rough with emotion.

Anna dabbed at her eyes with a handkerchief.

"Very touching," Chester B. Griffith said with the slightest mockery.

Liz watched Jace's jaw flex with sudden anger. She shook her head almost imperceptibly, then turned to the attorney.

"You're the main reason I asked everyone here today," Liz began. "If not for the lies you've been feeding me all along, I wouldn't be having these problems with Jace's family now."

Griffith reared up out of his chair in indignation. Liz could almost feel the tension radiating from Jace behind her, but because she'd extracted a promise from him earlier that he would let her handle this her way, he remained quiet and seated.

"You little ingrate," Griffith hissed. "Can't you see that *they* are the ones who've been lying to you?" Unconsciously he rubbed at his thigh.

"About what? You're the one who told me Goldie was involved in all those illegal activities. You're the one who implied that Giovanni was way up on the underworld totem pole. You're the one—" she glanced at Tony to gauge his reaction to her next comment "—who told Tony about the Ming vase."

"He did," Tony agreed. "He called me just the other day and said if I could get it for him, he would cover the expense of Sheila's operation."

"Oh, Tony!" Anna wailed.

Griffith sneered. "You always were a patsy, Tony, even when we were kids."

"Why you . . ." Tony flung himself out of his chair, but anticipating his reaction to Griffith's goading, Jace and Joe managed to restrain him. "Filthy bastard," Tony snarled. "You used me."

Griffith winced and took a step back. "So what? You didn't want Liz to have the vase any more than I did."

Tony sank into his chair, looking defeated and older than his years.

"I'll tell you 'so what,'" Liz said softly, taking a step closer to the lawyer. "I couldn't figure out why you were so upset when I told you I planned to give away all Goldie's money. I also didn't understand why you were so resistant to my knowing how everything was progressing. Then it hit me. You were placating me because you never intended to place those funds with the organizations I had stipulated or set up the trust funds for Goldie's grandchildren. And you thought I had the Ming, and you wanted that, too."

"Trust funds?" the Fabrizio clan cried in unison.

"Don't be absurd," Griffith said, ignoring them. "I've been following your instructions."

Liz shook her head. "It *looked* like you were doing what I'd asked, but it didn't feel right. I called a friend at the university who loves hacking. You know what that is, don't you? He can get into computers without anyone knowing. He called me back this morning with the information I needed." She leveled a look of disgust at him. "You diverted every penny Goldie left me into an account with *your* name on it. He even discovered you had one-way tickets to Switzerland for yourself and someone who's not your wife."

"That's ridiculous," Griffith protested. "I don't need your money."

"But you needed *Goldie's* money, didn't you? After liquidating her assets and transferring the cash into your own account, you would've really been set. The Ming was the icing on your greedy cake, and none of us would have been able to do anything about any of it once the funds were put into a Swiss bank."

Griffith stared at her in stony silence.

"You've planned this for years, haven't you? You ruined the relationship between Goldie and her children by perpetuating the lie that they wanted to have her committed."

"You idiot. You don't know what you're talking about."

Jace came out of his chair, with his two sizable uncles right behind him. "You insult Liz again, Griffith, and it'll be the last insult you make with a full set of teeth." Tony and Joe mumbled their agreement.

"You can't prove anything," Griffith snarled. "I have receipts from every agency you specified."

"I have no doubt you managed to forge those receipts somehow," Liz said before she parlayed her final thrust, "but I don't need to prove anything, Mr. Griffith. I have all the money back. Tony's wife will have her surgery, the grandchildren and great-grandchildren will have sizable trusts, and you have what you started with before you stole from me." She crossed her arms. "Computer hackers have such amazing abilities."

Griffith grimaced as he lunged forward a step.

Liz gazed pointedly at his right leg. "Hurt yourself, Mr. Griffith? I hope you got a tetanus shot for the dog bite." She lifted her eyes to his. "As a matter of fact, I'm not even sure Daisy's had her rabies shots yet."

The attorney turned an angry red, with veins popping out on his neck. Before anyone realized why he was reaching inside his suit coat, he had pulled out a lethal-looking revolver.

Anna squealed, but Jace and his uncles didn't make a sound, only watched Griffith with rage in their eyes. Griffith reached out and grabbed Liz, tugging her viciously against his body.

"Give it up, Griffith," Jace said with deadly calm. "You're not walking out of here with her."

"I either walk out with her, or she dies right now."

Liz had never believed a life could pass before a person's eyes in a matter of moments, but she felt as if that was exactly what was happening to her. The barrel of the gun clutched so tightly in Griffith's trembling hand chilled her skin where it made painful contact just below her ear.

She struggled to formulate a plan that would free her from his manic hold and keep Jace and his family safe, too. Unfortunately her brain had gone on standby, and all she could think about was the life she was never going to share with the man she loved.

Slowly, haltingly, Griffith began to back toward the front door. "I saw a vase on that table in the foyer," he said, his voice unrecognizable. "It's the Ming, isn't it?" He pressed the muzzle of the gun harder against Liz's neck, squeezing her arm savagely.

"No," Liz denied, improvising with, "That's just something I picked up at a flea market."

"Lying bitch!" he screamed, jerking her again. "You knew all along where it was, didn't you?" The gun skittered across her skin and discharged into the ceiling, leaving behind a red welt and powder burns.

Temporarily deafened by what sounded more like cannon fire than a gunshot, Liz swayed on her feet.

Jace lunged forward.

"Stay put, McGuinn. I won't think twice about killing your little whore now."

"You can't get us all," Jace told him, but he halted his forward momentum.

Griffith's backside butted up against the Shaker table.

From the top of the stairs came a low growl, then a sharp bark, and Daisy leapt over the risers. Caught totally off guard, Griffith momentarily released his hold on Liz. She seized the moment to make her escape, back-kicking his leg as she jumped away.

Griffith's howl of pain was music to her still-ringing ears. Jace pulled her to safety as Daisy sailed through the air, hitting the Shaker table before her open jaws closed around Griffith's arm.

The sugar cup crashed to the floor. Griffith screamed in agony and dropped his weapon as Daisy's teeth sank into his flesh.

Sure Liz and his mother were safe, Jace reached for the gun and pulled Daisy off her victim. His uncles subdued the whimpering lawyer.

The uniformed police officers who'd been waiting outside burst through the door.

"You do have a dog," was all Jace said.

Liz's ears were still ringing. In the confusion, she hadn't heard the vase fall and hit the floor. "Oh, no, look at the sugar cup!" she cried.

In appalled silence, everyone except the police officers stared at the priceless vase. It lay on the floor, splintered neatly into four shards.

With equal portions of dismay, regret and sadness, Liz lifted the pieces of the Ming and placed them on the Shaker table. Tears trickled down her cheeks.

Daisy nudged her leg in what felt like consolation. "I know, girl," Liz said, scratching behind the dog's ears. "Somehow you and that table were destined for a collision."

"I really thought the dog was a figment of your imagination," Jace said, coming up beside her when at last everyone had cleared out. He slid his arm around her waist, pulling her close against his side. "I think she deserves a T-bone steak for dinner."

Daisy looked up at him adoringly. Jace knelt to pat her and was rewarded with a lavish tongue-licking across his cheek. He grinned up at Liz. "I think she likes me."

"I'd say you've made another conquest."

Jace's blue blue eyes clouded with desire. "Are you saying you know someone else whose heart I've conquered?"

Liz reached out to run her fingers through his tousled hair. "Oh, I think I might be saying something along those lines."

He rose and pulled her into his arms, kissing her like she'd never been kissed before. "I thought I'd lost you," he groaned. "I couldn't have taken that, Lizzie. I love you."

"I love you, too," she whispered back against his lips. "Let's go upstairs and I'll show you how much."

"I'm sorry about the vase," Jace said, taking her hand.

Liz considered the four pieces, a wry smile tugging at her lips. "I am, too, but I don't suppose Mr. Griffith will want it now."

He continued to watch her uncertainly. "Probably not."

"I guess your uncle won't be wanting it anymore, either."

"I don't think he ever really did."

"With a little glue, I bet I could put it back together so the cracks don't even show."

"Mmm," he agreed.

Liz grinned at his solemn expression. "It'll probably be strong enough to hold two cups of sugar."

The next morning Daisy waited patiently at the bottom of the stairs until she heard the first stirrings from the bedroom.

With a final glance at the Shaker table, she turned and headed for the front door, her claws clicking against the floor. Her work here was done.

A moment later, Liz and Jace descended the stairs.

With eyes only for each other, they managed to make it to the bottom without mishap. Memories of the night before intruded with uninvited clarity and, as one, they looked toward the Shaker table.

Both were speechless as they stared at the sugar cup.

The night before there had been four delicate pieces. This morning there was a single perfect vase.

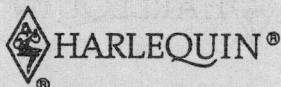

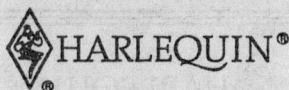

◈ HARLEQUIN®

MARRIAGE BY *Design*

Harlequin proudly presents four stories about *convenient* but not *conventional* reasons for marriage:

- ♦ To save your godchildren from a "wicked stepmother"

- ♦ To help out your eccentric aunt—and her sexy business partner

- ♦ To bring an old man happiness by making him a grandfather

- ♦ To escape from a ghostly existence and become a real woman

Marriage By Design—four brand-new stories by four of Harlequin's most popular authors:

CATHY GILLEN THACKER
JASMINE CRESSWELL
GLENDA SANDERS
MARGARET CHITTENDEN

Don't miss this exciting collection of stories about marriages of convenience. Available in April, wherever Harlequin books are sold.

MEN MADE IN AMERICA

Fifty red-blooded, white-hot, true-blue hunks
from every State in the Union!

Look for MEN MADE IN AMERICA! Written by some of
our most popular authors, these stories feature fifty of
the strongest, sexiest men, each from a different state in
the union!

Two titles available every other month at your favorite
retail outlet.

In March, look for:

TANGLED LIES by Anne Stuart (Hawaii)
ROGUE'S VALLEY by Kathleen Creighton (Idaho)

In April, look for:

LOVE BY PROXY by Diana Palmer (Illinois)
POSSIBLES by Lass Small (Indiana)

You won't be able to resist MEN MADE IN AMERICA!

Harlequin® Historical

LOOK TO THE PAST FOR
FUTURE FUN AND EXCITEMENT!

The past the Harlequin Historical way, that is. 1994 is going to be a banner year for us, so here's a preview of what to expect:

* The continuation of our bigger book program, with titles such as *Across Time* by Nina Beaumont, *Defy the Eagle* by Lynn Bartlett and *Unicorn Bride* by Claire Delacroix.

* A 1994 March Madness promotion featuring four titles by promising new authors Gayle Wilson, Cheryl St. John, Madris Dupree and Emily French.

* Brand-new in-line series: DESTINY'S WOMEN by Merline Lovelace and HIGHLANDER by Ruth Langan; and new chapters in old favorites, such as the SPARHAWK saga by Miranda Jarrett and the WARRIOR series by Margaret Moore.

* *Promised Brides,* an exciting brand-new anthology with stories by Mary Jo Putney, Kristin James and Julie Tetel.

* Our perennial favorite, the Christmas anthology, this year featuring Patricia Gardner Evans, Kathleen Eagle, Elaine Barbieri and Margaret Moore.

Watch for these programs and titles wherever Harlequin Historicals are sold.

HARLEQUIN HISTORICALS...
A TOUCH OF MAGIC!

HHPROM094